A SCATTERING

Emma Cameron

A CIP catalogue record for this title is available from the
British Library.

Published in the UK in 2021 by Emma Cameron

Cover design by Emily Mahon
Photo of Rannoch Moor © Daniel Kay/123rf.com
Bird illustration ©123rfanton

For Donald, Nancy and Sheila

1

ROSE

The sign on Jim's Café said closed. Rose peered through the window; red plastic chairs were piled upside down on tables and there was no sign of Jim or Dilara. At that time the place was usually full of workmen in hi-vis jackets talking quietly or reading their papers and an old man with a mound of buttered toast whom Dilara fussed over. Rose always ate breakfast in the café on studio days – a plate of mushrooms on toast and a mug of tea meant she didn't need to stop for lunch and it gave her time to think.

She stood outside Pak's Cosmetic Centre. Rows of heads in coloured wigs – vivid orange, shiny black and lime green – looked back at her. There was a new café further up the road serving coffee and croissants, which she didn't want. After a moment's indecision she went into the small supermarket and bought a packet of peanuts and some fruit. She was aware she'd been eating a lot of nuts since she'd become a vegan, but often there was no alternative.

She got back on her bike and cycled the familiar route to the studio, through the passageway behind the library, across London Fields under the huge plane trees, and over the cobbles by the garages, which were treacherous when wet. She locked her bike, climbed the two flights of stairs, put the key in the door and flicked on the light. Lee wasn't in yet but the room was spiked with the smell of oils and turpentine, rich and aromatic. Her latest work, a large painting of a factory with broken windows and a caved-in roof, was photo-realism but had the effect of a dystopian nightmare.

Rose had been making art in the warehouse for twelve years. At first she'd had a space that was small and dark – still, it was hers – then she'd been offered this, a large square with a wall of windows that gave a view over a raised railway where trains passed on their way to the City. It was a sanctuary, filled with a community of artists who shared tea, materials, gossip and exhibitions. Hackney was changing. She didn't want to see or admit it, had been walking around with blinkers on, but she knew it was true. Last year the post office had closed; it was now a restaurant. The shoe repair shop had become an estate agents – the second on the street.

She'd moved here after finishing art college, joining a housing co-op and being offered a small upstairs flat in a terraced house. She loved the area, the intrigue, the unexpectedness, the cultures mixing, colliding, collaborating – voices from Barbados, Ghana, Rajasthan, Chile, the Basque country. She liked the green spaces, Hackney Marshes, Springfield Park – a wide sweep of grass down to the river; ending up at the shabby café close to the water, where you could dream that London ended and the country began. She liked the secret places, curves, crannies, cut-throughs, churchyards, alleyways, estates and handsome houses.

Now cranes were moving up from the City, closer

and closer. New flats going up anywhere there was a spare patch of ground.

Rose dumped her bag on the table and went to fill the kettle, then pulled on blue overalls. Standing back, mug of coffee in hand, she surveyed the wall.

A sheet of paper, a metre square, was pinned on it. Waiting.

She had a degree in sculpture. Drawing was sometimes her first step towards three dimensions but could also be a piece of work in its own right. If the drawing wanted to move from the two-dimensional, she used clay. Pushing her fingers into the wet material, shaping it, rolling it, thumping it, was a satisfying, almost primeval, experience. Her subject matter was from her internal landscape and took abstract forms. People said they were reminded of mountains, craters, fantastical beasts. She would smile mysteriously, as if they could be right but equally they could be wrong, about her intention.

An idea emerged from deep in her subconscious. Opening a wooden box she took out a fat piece of charcoal, then moved closer to the paper and hesitated. A familiar fear surfaced. Maybe she'd forgotten how to do it; her idea would be insubstantial, only of interest to her.

She drew a large irregular circle in the centre. There.

Time passed. Voices murmured on a radio next door. She liked to know that someone was there, yet not disturbing her. The centre of the drawing was dark and heavy, the outer areas more textured, light, feathery crisscross marks made with a slender piece of charcoal. She had the sense that the piece was going to work.

Her mobile rang. The screen said Cal. She picked it up.

"Rosie?" His voice was high and strained. There was

the sound of traffic whooshing past.

"It's noisy – I can hardly hear you."

"I'm on the road."

"Where are you going?"

"To the coast."

Then she knew. It was 12 May – the anniversary of their father's disappearance.

Fear pulled at her.

"What are you going to do?"

"I don't......" Engine noise drowned out what he said next.

"Come back, Cal." But he'd already gone. She tried calling him back but it went straight to voicemail.

She remembered when she'd last seen him. They'd gone to see his friend's band playing. The band was getting a name and the venue was packed. They wove through the crowd and found a place to stand near the front. The lead singer, Cal's friend, had a beautiful voice. Although she wasn't a fan of indie music, Rose had enjoyed it.

Afterwards he'd said, "I loved that but it made me feel like shit," as he shivered and pulled the collar of his jacket up.

"You should believe in yourself, Cal."

"I'm thirty-four, Rosie, it'll be too late soon."

She'd watched him walk away, his shoulders hunched.

Unable to do any more work she packed up, calling in at Ridley Road market on the way home. Walking past the sad-eyed heads on the fish table she headed for her favourite fruit and veg stall, which was laid out like a painting; fat purple aubergines, red and orange peppers, plump cauliflowers and green leeks. She bought oranges, cucumber, tomatoes and celery. At home she made a salad, chopping everything neatly and putting it in a ceramic bowl, blue decorated with yellow fish. She made a dressing, adding mustard as a treat, then sat at the table by the window to eat. She was still thinking about Cal. Wondering what he was doing. It was unbelievable if he thought he could find something out after all this time.

The neighbour's children were playing in the garden. The older girl, Zaina, was running from one side to the other and Jaideep was trying to keep up. They were laughing.

Rose finished eating, did the washing up and then went to sit on the sofa with her art notebook.

The phone rang. Mum.

"It's Callum, he's had an accident. On the motorbike." An image of her brother's body, mangled, precious, leather clad.

Silence. Then, "How bad is it?"

"They're operating; it's his leg and something internal. I'm going there now."

"Where is he?"

"Colchester General. Alan's driving me."

"I'll meet you there."

On the train from Liverpool Street she looked out of the window, not wanting to catch anyone's eye, willing the train to go faster. Please don't let him die.

At the hospital reception she was told that Cal was out of theatre and had been transferred to the Intensive Care Unit. Walking down the long corridor her legs were stiff with fear.

Mum was sitting by the bed holding his hand, Alan hovering behind. Cal's arm was thin coming out of the sheet. The sockets of his eyes were dark. There was a drip

9

into his hand attached to a tube and a plastic pack dangling from a stand. He tried to smile when he saw Rose. He wasn't dead. She took a chair and sat on the other side of the bed.

Mum was looking pale and confused. "The doctors said they want to talk to me, so now you're here I'll go and find them."

Alan said he'd go with her.

When they'd gone Rose asked, "God, Cal, what happened? Were you going to Maldon?"

He nodded then looked away. "I want to understand what happened."

But the body under the waves wasn't releasing that information.

"Did you do it on purpose?"

"No," he tried to shrug and winced. "I saw the lorry but couldn't brake in time. I was going back to see if I could find someone who remembered him."

"It's nearly thirty years ago."

"There could be someone … anyway, the lorry got in the way."

"It's no good trying to work it out, Cal, it's impossible, you know that." She clenched her hands together.

"Don't be angry, Rosie."

He shut his eyes and looked to be in pain.

"Sorry, I'm scared, I don't want to lose you. We can't do anything about Dad but you can stay alive."

His eyes stayed shut and she put her hand over his. He didn't move it away. She sat quietly next to him, willing his mind and body to hold together. They were the same, she and him, always stuck in the past, needing answers.

She'd been five when he was born. Somewhere there

was a photo of the two of them, he a baby, sitting on her knee, she with her arms around him, both smiling. She'd loved his round face and black hair. He'd adored her too, followed her around, always called her Rosie; she didn't allow anyone else to do that. She worried about him, as if he was her child. For a few years Mum had worked in a supermarket, often long hours, and Rose was needed to help out with Cal. She took her responsibility seriously, walking with him to school every day. One time she'd looked away, distracted by children laughing behind her. He'd drifted towards the edge of the kerb and although she still had hold of his hand, he strayed close to the path of an oncoming van, which passed a metre or so away from his small body. Her heart had been in her mouth, not just for the thought of what could have happened to him, but also what her mum would have done.

He'd struggled at school and rebelled as often as he could. Later they found out he was dyslexic but by that time it was too late to get him help. Mum had found it hard to cope and Rose often tried to sort out the messes. When he left school he found the guitar and joined a band. For a few years he'd been happy but then, because he was always late for rehearsals, they'd thrown him out.

Mum and Alan came back. The doctors had told them that they'd put pins in Cal's lower leg and there was some damage to his spleen but this turned out to be bruising so he wouldn't need a further operation. They said he'd been lucky. He'd be transferred to an ordinary ward the next day if there were no complications.

It should have been a relief.

2

Rose was busy. She worked part time as a technician at an art college and the students were preparing for their degree shows. Cal was recovering and had started physiotherapy. He was to be discharged in a few days.

One evening she arrived home to find a parcel and card from Susan. "I've been clearing out the loft and found some things of your granddad's with a note addressed to you. Sorry I didn't notice it before."

Rose unwrapped the brown paper and found a battered cardboard box, a little larger than A4, tied with an old piece of string. She untied the knot and opened the lid to find several pieces of paper. On top was a note in Granddad's handwriting, dated June 2015, a month before he died.

> *To Rose,*
>
> *You are the only person I can leave these things to who might be interested in them. I hope you can make sense of the documents and that they will help you on your journey. If you don't know where you're from, you won't know where you're going.*
>
> *Love from Jack.*

"Jack", not "Granddad", seemed strange – it made the note more direct, less personal. She read it several times.

The words were clear and simple but they didn't make much sense. What journey? She wasn't sure it mattered where she came from.

Jack – her father's father. Rose's real grandma, Ruth, had died just before Rose was born and later he'd married Susan. An image of him – grey hair drifting onto his shoulders, old blue jacket with holes. Strong hands holding an axe above the upright log, bringing down the blade plumb in the centre, while she watched transfixed, knees locked together. He beckoning her over – Come and watch – she squealing and shaking her head. Walking through the mud around the harbour at low tide, pointing out the little bird figures busy at the water's edge, feeding off worms and grubs and tufts of weed. "Look, see the curlew and over there, wigeon, listen, you can hear the male calling," and she could: high-pitched, beautiful, as if it were crying for a lost soul mate. Footprints in the muddy sand ahead, her running to keep up with him. "Hurry along Rose or the wind will catch you, there's a storm coming." His voice – Canadian, soft. There was something stable and at the same time quite wild about him. The traumatic time he'd had in the war was etched on his face, indented and worn but still kind.

Rose placed the note on one side and picked out a small envelope. Inside there was a letter, folded tightly, which she opened with care. The paper was worn and cracked and covered with tiny, packed handwriting in black ink. It took her a moment to realise it was written in another language. Granddad had come from a Gaelic speaking area of Canada, the part known as Nova Scotia. He'd once tried to teach her the word for oyster-catcher. She tried to remember what it was, but after wracking her brains had to look it up. *gille-Brìghde*. She could almost hear the birds calling out their own names.

The next document was a sheet of paper folded in half – a hand-drawn family tree. She opened it out. It was different handwriting, looser, more scrawled, as if done in haste. The names were mainly MacGregors, who had married Camerons, Frasers or MacDonalds. Some had dates of birth and deaths, others were left blank or with a question mark. The dates were in the 1700s and 1800s. Underneath was a small brown leather book. The writing was the same as in the letter and again the language was not English. Some of the pages were torn and stained with water and dirt as if the book had been dropped and then recovered.

There was something else, covered in a piece of cotton. Carefully unwrapping the fabric, in case it was fragile, she found a stone. It was dark grey, almost black, patterned with white dots, smooth and worn, fitting in the palm of her hand. She turned it over and over, wondering whom it had belonged to.

The letter, the tree, the book and the stone.

History. She'd not been interested at school. Too many dates and kings and queens. She had learnt little of Scottish history. She was a MacGregor, a Scot by name, and that was all. She knew nothing of her past family, she had no stories and no photos, which had disappeared with her dad and granddad.

Smoothing out the fragile paper as much as she dared, Rose tried to decipher the words. The writing sloped to the right and blobs of ink dotted the page. She couldn't speak Gaelic and knew no one who could.

She wrote down the Gaelic words she could read,

leaving gaps for the others, then looked up their translation up online. There was no connection to English in the spellings and she imagined none at all in how they would sound. Uabhasach meant "terrible". How it was pronounced she didn't know.

> 'Pitlochry 1851. Dear Eòin ....letter from Ontario. It is long......... you. It was terrible......
> Torr Ua .... houses.... fire..... fathers bowl buried....... remember the MacGregors. The constables......beating and......attacks..... Màiri was injured.........Glasgow. I am..... Padair.......
> brother is dead.......... miss you and Seònaid.........
> my grandchild. Will I ever.......... I hope.........
> flourish..... my regards to Elizabeth and........
> thanks......their generosity. You loving mother Catrìona.'

She studied the page. Who was Catrìona? She was writing to someone in Canada. The event described sounded violent. 1851. There was a grandchild, so the writer must have been quite old when she wrote the letter. Looking again at the family tree, Rose found a mention of a Donnchadh marrying Catrìona in 1817. She counted five generations between herself and Catrìona.

An internet search for Torr Ua, which she thought must be a place, came up with nothing. Pitlochry was in Perthshire. She entered Torr Ua, Perthshire. A map from 1870 appeared showing a Loch Rannoch. To the north was some kind of settlement called Torr Uaine marked by the shape of rocks. Another search produced an earlier black and white map from 1839. The shapes were marked as rectangular in this, as if they were houses.

Between the years 1839 and 1870 something had

happened. The Highland Clearances came to Rose's mind; she knew the name but nothing about them. She did a search of the subject and found a small amount of information, which mainly stated that crofters were evicted to make way for sheep. The practice went on for about two hundred years.

With Cal in hospital and her own restlessness she wanted to know more but there was no one to ask. Dad had gone, taking his knowledge – if he had any – leaving behind a myriad of confusions.

Gone was the word she used – *disappeared* was what her mum said. No one said *killed himself* although they knew it was a possibility.

Mum and Dad had argued about the boat.

"It's only two thousand pounds, that's nothing for a boat, you and Rose and Cal can come sailing with me."

"You know I hate the sea, I'm seasick just looking at it," Mum had snapped, disappointing Rose, who was already on the horizon line.

He'd bought it anyway, spent a summer at the mooring near Maldon, making it seaworthy, then finally took his precious boat out on a maiden voyage. Other sailors had seen him, said he seemed unsteady on his feet, he was holding a bottle of something – whiskey? – as he boarded. The sea had been what they called a light swell, perfectly easy for a novice sailor. What was strange was that the boat was upright, anchor dropped. The body was never found; this was unusual they were told but it did sometimes happen. It wasn't clear whether he threw himself overboard, went for a swim and couldn't get back, or was caught by a rogue wave.

His disappearance came soon after Rose's tenth birthday

and she spent days, months, years, wondering if they'd ever find the body. Maybe he'd faked his disappearance to get away from them, you heard of people doing that. She couldn't decide if she preferred that story to the one in which he was so unhappy that he deliberately drowned himself. Both were unbearable.

For years afterwards she had a recurring dream. He was in a house at the bottom of the sea, saying it suited him to live among the fishes. She would wake up feeling that she couldn't breathe.

*

Cal was being discharged. The hospital said someone was needed to collect him so Rose went to Colchester. They took a taxi to the station, the train back to London and another cab to his place. When they got there, she saw how desolate it was. The walls were in need of painting. There was a large tea stain on the arm of the blue sofa. Cal's two guitars – one acoustic, one electric – were propped up against the wall.

She collected the mugs and glasses and put them in the sink. There was a dribble of washing up liquid which she squeezed into the bowl. The kitchen window looked out at a block of flats across a busy main road. The window frames were covered with a thick layer of black grit.

Cal manoeuvred himself on crutches into the living room and sat down with a grimace on the sofa, his plastered left leg stretched out in front. "I've got to keep this on for another four weeks. The worst thing is that my leg itches and I can't scratch it."

"Are you going to manage?"

"Of course. Laurie said I can ask her for help."

"You will be OK, won't you? I mean you're not going to do anything else."

"Like top myself?"

"Stop it Cal. Don't make jokes, I can't stand it."

He grinned. "It's alright, Rosie, I won't, I promise. Anyway, at least I haven't broken an arm, so I can still play the guitar. I've been thinking about it and I'm going to write some new songs, try to make a record. I've got lots of time now."

"While you were in hospital, I got a parcel from Susan with some of Granddad's things." She told him about the diary and Catrìona's letter and what she thought it might mean.

"I wonder what happened. Shame Granddad's not around to ask. Or Dad."

"I'm going to try and find out some more if I can. We know so little."

Rose began looking for a Gaelic translator. It seemed there weren't many and they were in high demand. Eventually she found a woman in Edinburgh called Bridget who said she could do the translation but it might take a few weeks.

It was a frenetic time at college. The degree show was going up and Rose had to deal with technical hitches and stressed and anxious students. As usual it all came together at the last minute and the work looked good. Then came the clearing up, the storing and throwing in skips of anything that couldn't be recycled. In late June she had a few weeks' holiday. She'd only been to Scotland once – to the Edinburgh festival – never any further north. It was time.

That night, as she was getting ready for bed, she looked

in the mirror. Her skin seemed even paler than usual. Red gold hair curled around her ears and across her forehead. Her eyes were dark brown, which people found surprising, expecting them to be green with her colouring. It was as if somehow God or genetics had got it wrong. She'd always had a sense there was something missing in her life; she put it down to the loss of Dad, or her lack of long-term partner, but here in this room she could tell it was more than that. A thread had been broken in her life, sometime long ago. It was time to follow it back.

She considered calling Mum to ask if she knew anything but decided not to, knowing what she would say – Oh Rose, you know I don't like talking about him – then Rose would feel bad, as if she was responsible for prodding at an old wound. Mum was with Alan now, she had slipped comfortably into his life, seemed happy. He had money and they lived in a beautiful half-timbered house in Suffolk.

Instead she called Cal. "Will you be OK if I go away for a week or two?"

"Of course. I've been looking after myself for years, remember we only see each other every couple of months, now you're always around. I have got some friends, you know. Where are you going?"

"To Scotland. I want to know exactly what happened. There's a reason that things aren't right – Dad, you and me, the rootlessness, our inability to settle. It's like we're always looking for something. I want to find what was lost."

She found her tent at the bottom of the wardrobe, went online and booked a room in a pub near the old village for a week, a train to Edinburgh and a hire car. Three days later she was on her way.

3

CATRÌONA

Catrìona lifted the pot of boiling water from the fire and carried it outside. She took several large pieces of lichen from her basket and crumbled them into the pot, stirring until it had all dissolved, then she dropped in a skein of cream wool. The smell of the dye, mixed with urine, rose up; strong and acrid but she didn't mind. Knew it was good. The threads turned bright yellow, the colour of gorse. She sang all the verses of *'An Bheinn Mhòr'* and by the end of the song the wool was exactly the colour she wanted. Lifting the skein with the spoon, she draped it evenly over the wall and left it to dry in the sun. Soon she would begin Mrs Patterson's shawl.

A breeze blew across the hillside; the day was cold but sunny. Snow still lay thick on the summit and slopes of Sìdh Chailleann. In the field behind the croft came the thump of Eòin's spade on the earth. Below, Jessie came out of her house and began to climb the hill. Eventually she reached the top.

"*Mhadainn mhath,* Jessie. Have you come to help me?"

"Yes, Mrs MacGregor."

Catrìona had long ago suggested that Jessie call her by her first name but the girl never would.

"I'm starting a new shawl today. The colours are dark

blue, pale green and yellow."

"It will be pretty," Jessie said.

She seemed more subdued than normal. When she visited Catrìona she liked to skip and dance, happy to be released from looking after the younger children. Instead she had her head down and was sniffing.

"Have you a cold?" Catrìona asked.

Jessie shook her head.

"What's the matter?" Still the girl did not speak. "Is your mother unwell?" Mairead had recently had a new baby and was still tired from the difficult birth.

"I'm frightened to say."

"Let's go inside. We'll sit by the fire and you can tell me."

They went into the house. The sun was shining through the small window, flames were licking at the peats, smoke spiralled up to the roof. They sat on wooden stools close to each other.

"We have a new teacher at school."

"That's right, Mr Holmes."

Catrìona had passed him on the road a few days ago, a small man, upright and stern looking. He'd nodded at her but there'd been no hint of a smile. She'd heard he was strict.

Jessie started talking, the words tumbling out. "Our last teacher, Mrs Dewar, let us talk how we wanted. Now we must only speak English. Mr Holmes said that Gaelic is for heathens and savages."

Catrìona sighed. She wasn't shocked to hear this. The ruling people had been trying to take their language for years.

"It's the way of things, Jessie, the teachers are in charge

at the school."

"The trouble is I forget and some words come out wrong."

Catrìona nodded. "It must be difficult to remember."

"Daniel answered a question – it was right but he said it in our language. Mr Holmes made him go and stand outside. Next day Mr Holmes brought a big wooden box into the classroom and told us that the next person who made a mistake was going to have to wear what was inside." Jessie stopped speaking and was looking pale in the firelight, as if a ghost had blown in on the wind.

Catrìona put her hand on Jessie's arm. "Go on."

"I kept staring at the box on the desk. I must have been nervous because when he asked me a Bible question I answered in Gaelic. He looked at me with a cold eye then beckoned for me to go to the front of the class. My legs were shaking as I left my desk. He took a key from his gown and unlocked the box. When he opened the lid we all gasped. Inside was a skull." Her small face was full of fear. She clutched Catrìona's hand. "Oh, Mrs MacGregor, it was a human one. There was a chain attached to the top and he hung it round my neck. He said I must wear it until the end of the day."

Catrìona was shocked. She'd heard tell of things like that happening in the north but never in their strath. "Oh my dear, that's very hard." She put her arms around Jessie, who leant against her and sobbed.

"I had to wear the skull all day. It was so heavy. The other children wouldn't speak to me and I felt ashamed. Now in the dark, when I try to sleep, I keep thinking I can see the horrible thing in the room. I'm so frightened."

"That was a cruel thing to do to a child. Have you told

your father?"

Jessie shook her head. "I am afraid he'd go to the school and kill Mr Holmes."

It was possible, Catrìona thought. Alasdair Fraser was known for his fierce temper, he had once been to jail for hitting a man who was offensive to Mairead. The family had grown even larger now and it would be very hard if he were sent away again.

She gave Jessie a hankie and told her to blow her nose. "Listen to me, child. This is what we'll do. We won't bother your mother and father because they have enough to worry them. Instead I'll talk to the teacher."

Jessie stopped sniffing and looked up. "Will you?"

"Yes, I promise. Now let's forget about Mr Holmes. Would you like some soup? It's turnip and kale and very tasty."

Jessie nodded, her face much brighter.

Catrìona ladled some soup into a wooden bowl and handed it to her. "I'm going to buy two more chickens soon to replace the ones the fox took, you can name them if you'd like?"

"Yes, can I?"

That evening, as Catrìona was threading the loom, she thought about her promise. She was worried about interfering in the affairs of education. She hadn't yet been formally introduced to Mr Holmes but if she waited there was a chance that Jessie would be made to wear the skull again. Jessie was young, only just twelve years old. She was a very clever girl; she could name all the birds by their song and all the wild flowers in the area. She could sing well and even recite some poems. Theirs was a language made for poetry and song, and it would be a pity if she became frightened of school and her education were to suffer.

The next day Catrìona waited outside the school until all the pupils had left. The teacher's office was just inside the front door. The nameplate was new. W.E. Holmes. She knocked once and waited. After a moment a voice called, "Enter."

He was sitting at a desk, the size of which seemed to dwarf him. Papers were spread in front.

"Good afternoon. I thought the person knocking must be a pupil who'd left something behind, there's usually one," he said. An English accent.

"Good afternoon, sir, my name is Catrìona MacGregor. I hope I'm not disturbing you?"

"Usually parents make an appointment but I expect I can spare a moment. Please take a seat." He gestured to the chair opposite. "What can I help you with?"

All the words she'd planned went out of her head. He was looking at her with a patient expression. She couldn't imagine him being so cruel as to hang a skull around a young child's neck. But Jessie had always been such an honest girl.

Catrìona took a deep breath and said, "My neighbour's child, Jessie Fraser, is dear to me, she's helped me out many times. Recently she's seemed frightened. When I asked her why, she told me that she was made to wear a human skull around her neck for speaking Gaelic in class." The words were out.

He studied her for a moment. "That's correct, Mrs MacGregor. It's the school's policy to make sure that pupils only speak the Queen's English. It's for their benefit. No child is going to progress if he, or indeed she, continues to speak that language. What they do at home is their concern."

He sounded polite but cold.

"I understand you want the pupils to learn English but I wonder if you could consider a lesser punishment. Jessie is at a young age. I'm worried that frightening her will affect her ability to learn."

He raised his eyes to the ceiling for a moment as if looking for guidance from God then asked in a pious voice, "Do you have the parents' permission to come here?"

She hesitated.

"They do know you're here?"

If Alasdair Fraser ever heard about what had happened the headteacher's life might be in danger, so she told a small lie. "I have their permission."

He raised his elbows to the desk and put the tips of his fingers together. "I've listened to your concerns but of course you must agree there can hardly be one rule for her and another for the rest."

She shook her head dumbly, wishing she had the courage to say that leniency should apply to all children, but she was afraid that she would anger him.

After a long minute's silence, he said, "I'm sorry but I cannot accept your request. Now please, I must get on."

Walking home, Catrìona hoped that even though Mr Holmes had refused her request he might think twice before unlocking the box again. A cool wind blew her shawl from her shoulder and she caught it and pulled it across her chest.

4

Seated at the loom Catrìona moved the shuttle deftly from side to side, humming to herself. The shawl was coming along. The green, blue and yellow looked well together. Mrs Patterson would be pleased.

Eòin came through the door, bending his head under the lintel. He'd grown tall in the last year and was looking more like his father, with his thick reddish-brown hair and large hands.

He put down his bag. "I've been to visit Seònaid, Mam."

"Is she well?"

He shook his head. "She's ailing. Her father is a cruel man. He wants her to do too much work – she must help with all the younger children, as well as milk the cow and cook the food. One evening she was so tired that she fell asleep in a chair. When he came home he pulled her up roughly and hit her. She showed me the bruises on her arms."

"Poor girl."

"I'm frightened for her, Mam." He was pulling off his jacket. "She told me he's done it before. All the walk home I was worrying."

He sat on a stool and warmed his hands at the fire. "Now I think I have the answer. I'll ask her to marry me. I want her to live here in Torr Uaine."

Catrìona rested the shuttle, surprised. "You're still young, Eòin."

"I'm twenty-one, I have a skill now. I can build us a new house. I love her."

"I know." She went and put a hand on his shoulder. "Her father may object."

His expression was determined. She remembered the look from when he was a small boy.

"It's not his business. Her mam likes me, she gives me extra food when I'm there and often asks when I'm to visit Seònaid next."

It seemed so recently that he was sitting on a stool in front of her, allowing her to untangle his hair when it grew too long. Now he was a grown man and considering marriage. She sighed and nodded. "Then if you're sure, you should go to see the factor about land. You'll need a home of your own."

*

The factor agreed that Eòin could rent a small portion of land.

"It's on the other side of the burn, higher up. He said it's the best he can offer me. It will be windy there but at least Seònaid will be safe and we'll be together."

Dressing in his best clothes and taking a small wooden horse that he'd carved, he went to visit Seònaid, returning later happy and excited.

"She's agreed. We told her mam, who gave us her blessing. She'll tell MacIntyre when it's a good moment. I'm going to start work on the house straight away."

Catrìona was beginning to accustom herself to the notion that her son was going to be married. Although he was young, he was strong and capable and had many skills.

When she arrived at the top of the hill the next day half the ground was already cleared and there were neat piles of rocks in four corners.

"I've been planning the design. The door and window will be facing Sìdh Chailleann. It will be the first thing we see when we get up. Do you think Seònaid will like it? She is used to being closer to the loch."

"Aye son, she'll be content here and when you're away working, I'll be here to make sure no harm comes to her."

The wedding date was decided on and the banns were read. Soon afterwards, Murdo MacIntyre came to the house. Catrìona heard him calling for Eòin outside the door. When she went to open it he was swaying on his feet. "That son of yours is stealing my daughter away, I will not allow it."

"Go home please, no good will come of this. Seònaid is old enough to make up her own mind. They love each other."

He laughed. "Love. Love. What good is that when you've got no one to help out with the bairns?"

Eòin must have heard the shouting because he came running from the field. "Are you alright, Mam?"

"You, you're not old enough to take care of her." MacIntyre spat the words out.

"I'm very well able. More so than you, I think."

"How dare you insult me?" MacIntyre rushed at Eòin with his fist raised and for a moment Catrìona thought he would strike but Eòin was too quick for him. He evaded the fist and MacIntyre slipped and fell in the mud. Catrìona almost felt sorry for him but remembered what he was capable of. He pulled himself to his feet, dirt covering the side of his face and shirt.

"You'll live to regret this," he said, then turned and marched away.

*

On a clear spring day, with only a few clouds hovering over the summit of Beinn Labhair, the people of the township came together, as they did whenever there was a house to be built.

The wooden couples for the A-frame were brought up the hillside by horse and cart and raised into place by Eòin, Alasdair, Daibhidh and other strong men. Stones had been gathered and arranged in piles. The people formed a chain, the strongest and ablest stood on their own and the less able in twos. They picked up the large stones first and began to pass them to the front of the queue, to those who had laid a house before. These stones formed the first supporting row. Once they were laid they used the medium-sized stones for the next row. Smaller stones fitted in the gaps. Finding the right one was a skill. Catrìona worked alongside Jessie who, although she was slender, could pick up a weight. They sang as they laboured, following the rhythm of the swing of the stone from hand to hand, with words that had been heard in the strath for centuries. Catrìona held herself as upright as she could so that she didn't succumb to back pain.

By the end of the morning the walls had three levels of stone. There was a solid gap for the door and Eòin had marked where he wanted the window. They took a break to eat. Her cousin Padair came and sat by her. She was pleased to see him.

"Are you keeping well, Catrìona?"

"Aye, I'm as fit as can be expected."

"When you get to my age you'll be feeling it."

Padair was eight years older than her. She noticed that he was more stooped than usual and wondered whether the work he did was too much for him. He laboured for a farmer near Pitlochry as well as keeping his own croft going. Eleanor was ailing and couldn't help out as much as she used to.

"I am happy that Eòin is making a new family. He's doing well at the workshop, I drop in there sometimes to talk to Lachlann and hear only good about him."

"He works very hard. I hope that now he has Seònaid with him he'll be happy."

Padair nodded. "You've done a good job. He'll stay close to you, unlike my boys. Much good it's done them. They thought they would be rich in Edinburgh and Glasgow but it isn't the way."

Catrìona recalled that his sons had left home within a year of each other – one to work in the mines, the other in a mill in Glasgow. They could write but they hardly ever did and they had come home only once, at Christmas three years ago, looking grim faced and with few gifts for the family.

After a rest the villagers began work on the last row of rocks. Catrìona's arms and back were aching. She insisted that Jessie go home. "You've done enough now, child."

The sun was starting to set as the final row was completed. Those that were left stood back to admire their work. The walls looked sturdy, six rows of stones high, A-frame standing firm at each end.

"It's solid," said Padair. "It will keep out the winter storms. You'll raise strong sons and daughters here."

Eòin ducked his head and looked pleased.

Màiri came up the hill to look. "When the roof is on I'll make you a special bunch of herbs and flowers for you to hang over the hearth, it will cleanse the house ready for you to move in."

"Thank you, Aunt Mhàiri," Eòin said, "I'd like that."

The villagers trudged back down the hill to their own houses. Padair took his leave. They hugged and said they would be seeing each other soon.

Catrìona was collecting her things ready to go when Eòin tapped her on the shoulder. "Wait," he said.

He took something from his pocket and held it in his palm for her to look at. "I found this in the wall of our house." It was an oval shaped stone, smooth and perfect. The dark surface was covered in a pattern of silvery white dots.

"I wanted something to remind me of you, my father and my sisters." He held it in his hands, then slotted it into a space by the side of the doorframe.

She touched his cheek. "Thank you, son."

*

It was a busy time of the year and much would need to be done to prepare the ground for planting. The days leading up to the wedding passed quickly. Although Seònaid had said that she only wanted a few people there and no big feast, fearing her father would get drunk and cause trouble, still it was important to make sure it was a happy day.

Catrìona wove a special piece of cloth to be made into

a waistcoat for Eòin, dark green patterned with thread the colour of heather. She treasured the final days of him being in the house – listening to his easy breathing in the box bed nearby and his cheerful greeting in the morning. Her job had been to help him grow, teach him about harvests and how to use and mend and care for all their tools. Now it was done. He was skilled and had work in the carpentry workshop in Kinloch, making and mending furniture. He would make a fine husband for Seònaid.

One morning in the field she stood for a moment looking out across the strath. It was cold and although she was warm from working, a shiver went through her body. She no longer had a purpose. She had no husband and her son was grown. She was old and no use to anyone. Her time would soon be over. Then she heard Mairead calling to her boys in the field below and she bent again to her digging. Those were foolish thoughts, for someone with far too much time on their hands.

On a breezy, showery day in April, Seònaid and Eòin were married at the kirk in Killichonan. Seònaid looked lovely in a white cotton dress with blue ribbons in her black hair and a bouquet of wild flowers that Catrìona had picked for her. Eòin was wearing his best suit and the new waistcoat looked very well.

Although the kirk was almost empty the ceremony was special and as the couple said their vows Catrìona began to cry. Next to her Màiri, who was never prone to sentimentality, was sniffing too. A few mothers and children were there to wave as they came out. Catrìona caught a glimpse of MacIntyre, standing under the yew tree, face like thunder, but he did not speak or try to approach them. Seònaid didn't notice; she was busy trying to stop her dress from trailing in the mud as she climbed onto the trap.

5

ROSE

Rose loved driving. Turning west off the A9 north of Edinburgh the countryside grew wilder and more beautiful. After about three hours she arrived in Kinloch, a small village at the east end of Loch Rannoch. She drove along the main street and found the Rannoch Inn at the far end.

Inside, a man was putting away glasses; he looked round as she entered. He had thick brown hair and a friendly, bearded face.

"Hello there."

"Hi. I'm Rose. I booked a room."

"Aye. Welcome to Kinloch. I'm Angus. Where've you come from?"

"From London."

He nodded. "A fair way. I'll put you in a room at the back of the pub; the other one is over the bar. It might get a bit noisy later, we've got a music and poetry night. We do food if you're hungry?"

"Thanks. I am."

He showed her to the room, which was small but had a view across the loch to mountains beyond. The light on the water was silver and there were ripples catching the last pink from the sky. It was beautiful; but still, as she stood looking out of the window, she had a flash of uncertainty about why she was there. Chasing dots on a map. It could be the place Catrìona had spoken about in the letter but maybe it wasn't. Maybe she'd come all this way and spent a lot of money on a useless whim.

From downstairs came the sound of voices and occasional bursts of laughter, then fiddles tuning up. She hadn't eaten since breakfast and was hungry. Caught between feeling it was an adventure and that, somehow, she was an intruder, she went downstairs. Angus was behind the bar, and Rose ordered a salad sandwich and a red wine. The bar was almost full but she found a seat by the window. A young woman sitting nearby smiled and said hello, as did an older couple at the next table. As she watched and listened, she could hear Scottish accents and an occasional foreign tongue.

The atmosphere was lively and full of expectation. Musicians were gathering in the centre of the room, chatting. After a while some moved to the side, leaving a man with a fiddle, one with a pipe and a woman with an accordion. The fiddle player gave a nod and they began to play, slowly at first, gradually building up the pace, faster and faster, fingers flying over their instruments. Rose couldn't believe they could play that quickly. Suddenly they stopped. They took a collective breath, then laughed. Everyone clapped.

A young woman in a blue dress stood up and began to sing – a high, beautiful voice. The song was sad, about a lost love. Rose watched as the fiddle player raised the instrument under his chin and began to play along. Dark curly hair fell across his forehead. The expression on his face was serene but his eyes were focussed. The song finished and two older women stood to render a jaunty ditty a cappella. Although Rose couldn't make out all the words, it seemed to be mainly about sex.

She noticed an old man in a corner, blue cap pulled low over his face, gazing into the fire, warming his hands. He appeared to be lost in the flames. Someone tapped him on the shoulder and leaned down to speak. He nodded and when the women had finished the old man stood and walked slowly to the centre of the room. Clearing his throat, he shut his eyes and began to sing. Rose strained to make out the words then understood that he was singing in Gaelic. He had a deep voice, sonorous and hypnotic. The song took hold of her, seeming to infiltrate her body, striking something inside and resonating. It was a strange feeling, as if she knew the words, or had known them long ago. She wished he would go on singing but after one song he stopped and went back to his seat. Rose remembered the diary in her pocket. Unsure whether it was OK, she hesitated for a moment then stood and walked over to sit near the old man.

"I liked your song."

He was gazing straight ahead and didn't seem to hear at first, then he turned towards her. His eyes were a clear pale blue, watery and reddened round the rims.

"Do you come from this area?"

"Aye."

His brevity made her feel awkward. She tried again. "May I ask you something?"

He studied her as if trying to make up his mind.

"Sorry lassie, I'm no in the mood for questions."

It wasn't unkind, just dismissive.

"Oh sorry, I didn't mean to bother you." Rose got up

and went back to her seat, upset with herself. She'd only just arrived and had already put her foot in it. After a few minutes the old man went to the bar, put his glass down, then turned and walked out without a backward glance.

Finishing her wine, Rose resolved to go back to her room. She picked up her bag then noticed that the fiddle player was walking towards her. He gestured to a spare seat at the next table.

"May I?"

She nodded and he sat down.

The fiddle player smiled. "Are you enjoying the music?"

Rose put her bag down. "Yes, it's wonderful. I loved the Gaelic song."

"Aye, that's Seumas, he's amazing."

"I wanted to ask him something but he left."

"He's not always that sociable. Are you on holiday?"

"Not really. I'm looking for something."

"What's that?" He looked interested. He had a serious face, with a touch of something sad about it.

"A place. It's called Torr and a word beginning with U. I'm not sure how to pronounce it."

He thought for a moment then nodded. "You must mean Torr Uaine? It's an abandoned village not far from here."

"That must be it. I read about it. I'm an artist, I like unusual places."

She didn't want to try to explain about her family.

"It's on the north side of the loch, there's a narrow track just before the turning into Creag Dhubh Lodge. It's about half a mile up the hill."

"Thanks."

"I'm Tòmas by the way."

"I'm Rose." They shook hands briefly and both laughed at the slightly awkward exchange.

His friend called over, "We're starting."

He got up. "Hope you find it. Maybe see you another night." It was said casually but as if he meant it.

Rose went to bed soon after, tired from the travelling, and fell asleep to the sound of the music below.

She woke early and after a shower went downstairs. To the side of the bar was a conservatory where there were several tables. Through a line of trees she could see the loch. A low white mist hung over the water.

One place had been laid for breakfast; it seemed she was the only guest. A middle-aged woman came through a minute later.

"Hello, good morning, you must be Rose."

"Yes, that's me."

"I'm Shona. Now, what would you like to eat? We have porridge or a cooked breakfast."

Rose asked for porridge made with water.

"Have you plans for today?"

"I'm going to explore the loch and maybe have a walk."

"When the mist clears it should be a fine morning."

After breakfast Rose studied the map. The loch appeared to be about ten miles long with a narrow road running around the circumference. The track to Torr Uaine that Tòmas had mentioned was on the north side. She headed out.

From the pub she took the road along the north shore. It was narrow, with occasional passing places, but there were no other cars. After about five miles she noticed a turning and pulled onto a verge at the loch edge to check the map. The track looked right – on a slight bend in the road.

She took her backpack and began walking up the stony track. After about a hundred metres she passed a large barn, which was empty – there were no houses and no one around. She began to ascend, passing a copse of birch trees, their elegant heart-shaped leaves rustling in the breeze. As she climbed the view became panoramic. To the south a cone shaped mountain rose from the hills, to the west were forests and, in the distance, high mountains.

After a while the path veered to the left. The village was further than she'd imagined. She was out of breath, unaccustomed to climbing, and had a slight worry that maybe she'd gone the wrong way. She sat on a wall to catch her breath and check the map again. It seemed that she was on the right track but still had a little further to go. She set off again and soon came to a high fence with a gate. At first she thought it was locked but on checking she realised the padlock wasn't set. There were no cattle in the field so she slid the bolt and went through. The track continued through springy heather. She passed a low wall. Behind it was a metal trap in which a small creature, maybe a stoat or a pine marten, had been caught. Its mouth was open and it looked as if it had died in pain. She turned away.

Ahead of her, spread across the hillside, were mounds of stones. As she got closer the outline of a house became clear. The remains of stone walls, with grass growing up the sides. She walked round, taking in the shape – a long-sided rectangle. There was a gap, which must have been for the door. Inside the ground was lumpy with fallen stones – there was no evidence of any furniture, or any living thing.

Further up was another house and there were more, scattered over the hillside on either side of a burn. Rose walked down to the water, which was fast flowing with deep pools. Looking for a place to cross she came to a wide shallow spot and placing a foot on the stone in the centre jumped over the rushing water. The slope on the other bank was steeper. She climbed to the top and, sitting on a large boulder close to one of the houses, she surveyed the grey skeleton of the village. Despite how warm she was from walking, she shivered. It was a remote place. There was little shelter and there must be snow in the winter this high up. The houses had been built close together, only a couple of metres between some of them, maybe to give protection from the weather. Altogether she counted at least twenty buildings. Sixty or more people could have lived there; possibly her relatives had been among them, but now there was no sign of anyone. It was as if they'd been swept away, along with all their possessions.

She wandered around each of the stony outlines and then choosing one she went inside. Again the ground was bumpy, with grass covering the fallen rocks. There was a sense of peace but also of emptiness, people gone, along with their stories. She thought about the letter. Catrìona had mentioned a bowl buried nearby but there was no way of telling which house was hers. She took the stone from her backpack and placed it on top of the wall. It was the same kind, dark grey, patterned with white.

The wind was starting to swirl around the hillside and the clouds, which had been white, were now grey. She would have liked to do a drawing but it looked like it was going to rain. She took some photos with her phone instead then zipped up her jacket. It was time to go.

Rose walked back down the track. A fine drizzle was beginning just as she reached the car.

She drove around the circumference of the loch, crossing a bridge at the far end, passing an occasional cluster of houses and a new build. She drove across the bridge at the far end of the loch and around the south side which seemed to be even less populated. Although the scenery was beautiful the overwhelming sense was one of isolation.

*

That evening the pub was quiet. Angus told her there would be more visitors when the school summer holidays started.

She received an email from Bridget, with a document attached. "This is the first part of the diary. Some is hard to decipher. Will send you more as soon as I am able."

> **February** *The hills are white with frost. Mrs MacClaren's shawl is finished and sent by parcel. A fox has taken two chickens.*
> *Eòin and I have begun digging the field. It is hard with frost. My back aches from pulling the harrow. Soon I will begin Mrs Patterson's shawl.*
> *Jessie is having difficulties at school through no fault of her own.*
> *The teacher says that in the classroom all pupils must speak the Queen's English.*
> *I am baking Màiri an oat and honey cake.*
> **March.** *Eòin and Seònaid are to marry. Eòin says her father beats her.*
> *Daibhidh is helping me in the field. The first turnips and potatoes are planted. The wind blows hard. I fill the gaps around the door with heather.*

Rose read this through several times. She could clearly picture Catrìona in the village on the hillside, busy with her work, surviving the wind and the Highland winters. Eòin and Seònaid were mentioned in the letter – perhaps Jessie was a younger daughter.

How different it seemed to her own comfortable, twenty-first century life in a large city surrounded by buildings with central heating and cars and technology. She thought about her granddad in his house in Brightlingsea. He was very good at growing things. There were always leeks and carrots and potatoes in the ground and apples on the trees in the long narrow garden. Something of the rural had been in his blood.

She wanted to know more. She longed for a sense of how Catrìona and the other crofters had lived. It was time to put the tent to use and get closer to the land. She'd read that wild camping was allowed in Scotland. In the local shop she bought teabags, peanut butter, bread and a tin of soup. She'd paid for the room for a week and told Angus she'd be back after a couple of nights. Packing the car, she drove to the place where the track began.

Again the gate was unlocked and she made her way into the village. Above the burn was a house with four rows of stone remaining which would provide some protection from the wind. The ground inside was damp but not waterlogged. She pitched the small tent, siting it so that the opening faced the mountains.

She was intrigued by the buried bowl mentioned in Catrìona's letter and had bought a small garden fork from the shop to do some excavating. Beginning with the house she was camping in she began digging just outside the door. She pulled away the grass, which was thick and compacted, and dug a hole several centimetres deep but found nothing there. She moved to a house higher up, located the door and began another search but again there was no sign of a wooden object. She tried one more dwelling then stopped. There were too many houses and anyway the bowl would probably have disintegrated by now.

The sun was starting to sink over the mountaintops. Granddad had once or twice shown her wild plants in the hedgerows that could be eaten. She remembered names: nettle, borage, dandelion. She began a search of the hillside and came back with a handful of leaves. She lit the small camping gaz stove, set a pan of water to boil and dropped the leaves in, stirring and adding salt. Sitting on the wall she ate a peanut butter sandwich and drank the soup. It tasted delicious.

Rose was beginning to get a sense of how it might have been to live in that place, surrounded by such wild beauty. The sun went down, streaks of pink stretching out like tendrils under jagged grey clouds. Purple heather surrounded her, glowing almost fluorescent in the twilight. On the horizon of the hill she could see the outline of several deer.

When the fire had died to embers, she unrolled the sleeping bag and climbed inside. A breeze rippled the outside of the tent but she was warm and the grass was soft. In the tent she held a torch over her book, *The Gaelic Poets*. Choosing a page at random she began to read aloud.

Còmhlan bheanntan, stòiteachd bheanntan,
còrr-lios bheanntan fàsmhor.....

The translation, which she glanced at, was on the opposite page but it was the sound of the words that gave her most pleasure.

In the night she woke, needing to piss. As she unzipped

the tent she caught a glimpse of an animal jumping down from a wall, a wide, striped tail flicked upwards in defiance. A half moon was shining over the loch. Stars crowded in the sky, layer upon layer of silver points, arching above her head. As she stared up, a sense of connection to the vast universe took hold of her. She wanted to reach out and speak to it – *I am part of you and you are part of me.*

Light filtering through the tent woke her in the morning. The sun was rising at the side of the cone-shaped mountain which the map told her was Schiehallion. Although she was a long way from London and no one knew exactly where she was, Rose didn't feel lonely. It was as if the land had opened up to allow her in. Outside the tent she stretched her arms and back, glad to be released from the confines of the sleeping bag. Despite not having slept in a proper bed she felt rested.

Taking her towel she made her way down to the burn, to a place where water cascaded over rocks into a deep pool. It was hidden from the track so she stripped off her clothes and waded in, the cold making her gasp. She scooped handfuls of water over herself, letting it pour over her shoulders and breasts, imagining all the women who had done so before – wondering if Catrìona had looked anything like her, the same tall, narrow frame and reddish hair. She dried herself, enjoying the tingling of her skin as it began to warm. Back at the tent she drank hot tea. There must have been days like this when life could be lived outside. She tried to imagine the games the children had played and the songs they'd sung, their voices echoing across the glen.

It was a still morning, the early light was soft and clear. She took out her paints and sketchbook and began to draw a small group of the houses, focussing on the textures and patterns that she saw in the landscape of stone, grass and heather. After making several pencil sketches she began a watercolour, a pale wash for the sky and a darker one for the land. She mixed ochres, greens and purples for the colours on the hillside, investigated the reflections in the loch and the limpid quality of the blue sky. The painting was neither completely realistic or abstract – it was an evocation, an attempt to capture her relationship with the landscape in that moment and find the spirit of Catrìona's life there.

Later Rose restarted her search for the bowl. There'd been a shower in the night and the ground had softened, making digging easier. She chose a house at random, slightly higher than the others. Buried under a large flat stone at the side of the house she found a piece of wood. It was a smooth oblong shape, charred and rotten at one end. She held it up and recognised it as a shuttle, used in handloom weaving. Someone had been making cloth. It was the first evidence, other than the houses, of people living there.

As she examined it, she heard the sound of an engine revving as it came up the hill. It went past but then suddenly the noise stopped. She waited, hoping whoever it was would move on, but a car door slammed and a man appeared on the hill above. He began to descend towards her and sensing trouble she dropped the fork and the shuttle. He stopped a few yards away. She saw he was carrying a shotgun, which he held at his side.

At the sight of the gun she tensed, clenching her hands into fists.

He said, "What are you doing here?"

45

"I'm camping for a couple of days." She tried to sound casual.

He walked around and spotted the hole.

"The owner doesn't allow camping, especially in the summer – there could be fires. You need to pack up and go."

Although she was tall, he was much broader than her. She'd been used to the smells of the earth, the wet grass and the bracken. Now she could smell the sweat of another human being whose intentions weren't necessarily good.

She swallowed. "I'm only staying one more night."

He pointed to the bare earth. "That's damage."

"I'll put the turf back, it will regrow. I know I'm allowed to camp, I've read about it."

"I make the rules here." He shifted the gun so it was across his body.

She wanted to stand her ground but there was no one to help her or to be a witness if anything happened so she began to take down the tent. Aware he was watching, she struggled to pack neatly, her actions made clumsy by fear. He didn't say a word. The silence was oppressive. When she'd finished she hitched the rucksack on her back, not looking at him for fear of what she might see in his face, then started making her way up to the track.

"Don't come back."

*

The man's malevolent intervention had wrenched Rose from a place of calm. She walked down the hill, shaken and, at the same time, angry, with him and with herself, for not standing up to him. It began to rain, large drops splashing on the stones, causing them to become slippery.

Her backpack felt heavier than it had done, despite the fact that there was little food and water in it.

On the way down she walked through a field, avoiding the track, fearing he would overtake her. At the bottom she came across a large wooden structure covered in wire mesh, a kind of cage. Inside, on the ground, was a long creature covered in fur and blood, which might be a hare. Above was a bird, flying from one side of the cage to the other, clearly terrified. She caught a glimpse of a golden yellow eye and thought it could be a hen harrier. They were beautiful and endangered. Several feathers lay on the ground, as if fear was causing the bird to destroy itself. Trying to work out what she was witnessing, Rose stepped back and noticed the sign which read, "This is a legal trap." Below was a name and a telephone number.

She looked around to check that no one was watching her then, trying to suppress her fear, she began to examine the cage.

The roof was a sloping v-shape with a gap in the centre, which must have been how the bird got in. It would be impossible for it to get out. The mesh door was padlocked. She examined the lock, which was small but new and would need bolt cutters to remove it. One of the door hinges was rusty and loose. She remembered the garden fork and, taking it out of the bag, forced it between the frame and the hinge and pushed hard. The bird flapped its wings in terror. She spoke to it in as calm a voice as she could manage. "It's alright, I won't hurt you, I promise."

Her heart was beating fast. Any moment the gamekeeper could return. She worked on the lower hinge first and then the one above. They started to give. When both were loosened she took hold of the doorframe and pulled with all her strength. The door broke away and fell to the ground. She stepped away. The bird fluttered from side to side then flew straight out through the opening. It went low over the ground then up and over the tops of the trees until she lost sight of it.

Exhausted, as if she too had been struggling to escape, Rose made her way back to the track. A black 4x4 was coming up the hill towards her. She froze for a second then forced herself to keep walking; if it stopped and anyone questioned her she would deny everything. The vehicle passed her; there were two men inside, but although they glanced at her curiously, they didn't appear to notice the damaged trap.

Back in the car she sat for a while, her hands shaking from the effort of breaking the cage. The casual cruelty of the trap found in such a beautiful place hurt like a sharp knife in her body. She rested her head and arms on the steering wheel, trying to block out the image of the bird and the hare and to steady her breathing. At least the bird might survive.

After a while she started the engine and continued driving west by the loch. Noticing a large grey house set back from the road she stopped the car and got out. In front of the building was a wide swathe of grass sloping gently down to the loch. A sign on the gatepost said "Creag Dubh. Private." The house was vast, almost like a whole village.

She heard a noise and turned. Coming towards her on a bicycle was a young woman with long hair. As she got closer the front wheel appeared to hit a stone, the bike swerved and the woman toppled into the ditch.

"Shit," she said, pushing the bike from her and

standing up.

"Are you OK?" Rose said.

"Just about." She looked down at her trousers, which had a smear of mud on them. "God, that's all I need. Too late to go back and change."

"Are you going to work?"

"Yes, in there," she said pointing to the house. "I'm meant to look clean if not smart." Her thick blonde hair looked unruly, threatening to break out from its clip.

"What are they like? The people."

The young woman looked at Rose, as if trying to work out why she was so interested.

"It's just such a big house. I wondered who owned it."

"The Menzies. They own all of this." She gestured to the land around them.

"Including the deserted village up the hill?'

"Oh, you've been there? Yes, and that. Anyway, I better get going or I'll be late as well. They've got a big party arriving tonight."

"Maybe I'll see you again. I'm Rose. I'm staying round here for a few days."

"I'm Aileen, I live over there." She pointed to the far end of the loch.

"I hope they don't notice the mud."

"Thanks. So do I. See you." She got back on her bike and cycled to the gate entrance.

Rose turned the car and drove, thinking about the abandoned village – its bleakness and beauty – the bird trap, the huge house; the fact that there were almost no people anywhere. The rain had stopped and there was sunshine glistening on the dripping trees and the surface of the loch. It seemed that here the weather changed every hour or so.

Back at the pub she revelled in the hot shower. The experience with the gamekeeper and bird trap didn't seem so bad now she was with people again. Later she went down for something to eat. There were a few people in the bar including Tòmas who was in a corner seat with a pint and a sandwich. He waved when he saw her. "Hi Rose, how are you doing?"

She went over to where he was sitting.

"You found the village?"

"I camped there last night. It was amazing. I could sense a spirit there."

He nodded. "It's unusual to find a whole village intact. Mostly all you see is the outline of a house or some scattered rocks."

"I would have stayed longer but a man came along and told me to go. He was big and had a gun."

"That sounds like Fergusson, the gamekeeper. He can be unpleasant and he pushes things to the limit."

"There was something else. I found a cage. There was a bird, a hen harrier I think, caught in it."

"Those traps are meant for crows, which are classed as vermin. They often end up trapping other birds. The landowners manage the area for grouse shooting and deer stalking – sport."

"How can anyone think that's sport?" Rose was aware she knew nothing of the place and its customs but her hatred of animal cruelty ran deep.

"People do and it's an employer round here – many believe in it."

"You don't though?"

"God no, I hate it. We're trying to change things, find

other ways of using the land, but the Menzies are secretive, they never engage with any of us."

"Anyway, I broke the trap and let the bird out."

He looked at her, surprised. "Did you? Don't tell anyone else that – you could get in trouble."

"It was losing feathers – I was worried it would die."

"I'm glad you did it but be careful."

She thought it best to change the subject.

"Do you come from this area?"

"I was born in Perth but my mum and dad split up when I was young and me and Mum moved to Edinburgh. I grew up there. I came back here a few years ago, when things… changed."

"It's a beautiful area."

He nodded. "And what about you?"

"I live in East London. It's a great place to be an artist. Well, it was, anyway."

"Was?"

"Gentrification. It's changing everything, the artists are starting to disappear, along with the people of the global majority and other cultures. All the things I liked about it in the first place."

"That doesn't sound good. What kind of art do you make?"

"I'm a sculptor but I do a lot of drawing too. I did some sketches of Torr Uaine, actually."

"I'd love to see them."

She smiled, embarrassed. "Maybe, sometime."

"What will you do now?"

"I want to stay a bit longer, try to find out what happened to my ancestors."

"There are one or two people around here who might

know things. Seumas Fraser – he's been here the longest. He's worth talking to if you can. It might be tricky though. He keeps himself to himself; prefers animals to humans."

"I don't think he wanted to talk to me."

"There might be a way. Aileen, a friend of mine, she knows him well."

"I met someone called Aileen earlier. She was going to work at the estate."

"Aye that's her. Maybe she'll go with you to see him."

6

Aileen lived at the west end of the loch, in a small cottage set among a small cluster of other cottages, all of which had maroon-coloured woodwork.

She came to the door when Rose knocked. "Hi, Rose. Come in. Sorry about the mess. I've been working a lot, no time to clear up after Lily."

The living room was covered in toys.

"How old is she?"

"Eight, nearly nine. She's growing up really fast. Have a seat." She gestured to a small orange sofa.

The room was full of colour. A piece of stained glass hung in the window, ruby red and blue catching the light, a yellow blanket was draped over a chair and there was a multi-coloured rug on the floor.

"This is a lovely place."

"We're only renting, that's the way of things round here, the estate own everything. Ruaridh, my partner, works in the Cairngorms on a rewilding project, he comes back at the weekends. I love it here, it's really quiet and wild still but there's a lot of cultural stuff happening in Aberfeldy. The only problem is there's not much work and no secondary school nearby. In two years, Lily will have to go even further for school."

"That sounds hard."

She nodded. "It will be. So what do you want to

ask Seumas?"

"I'm interested in the deserted village, Torr Uaine. I'd like to know more about its history."

"If anyone can help you it's Seumas, he's lived here the longest. I've got some homemade bread we can take him, see if that will loosen him up. I don't think he eats much so I bring him food from time to time."

"Thanks for offering to do this."

"That's OK, I like listening to his stories and underneath he has a good heart. We'll go in my car then I can bring you back here after."

They drove along the loch to the Black Wood. Seumas's house was set back into the trees. It was built of old grey stone, with a dark green wooden porch; patches of sunlight decorated the roof. To the side were two wooden buildings, one full of stacked logs, the other bits of machinery and tools.

As they approached the door it opened and a small brown dog came running out barking. It leapt up at Aileen, tail wagging. "Hello Barney, good boy."

The door opened wider and Seumas appeared in the threshold.

"Hello Seumas."

"Aye, there you are, Aileen, and who is this with you?"

"This is Rose. She says you met in the pub a few days ago."

He nodded. "I remember."

"We've brought you a loaf of bread."

"Thanks lassie. I was about to go for my walk so I'll just put this inside and then you can join me."

He came back out carrying a walking stick. He was a medium height, thin, wearing a thick shirt over corduroy trousers and wellingtons.

"We'll go this way." He pointed to the right fork. "I like to vary the route so I can keep check on the boundaries – make sure those Menzies aren't encroaching."

"Seumas is the caretaker of the wood," Aileen said.

"Unofficial. The Forestry Commission own the land but I take care of it. This wood is a remnant of the ancient Caledonian forest. Full of wildlife – crossbills, woodpeckers, pine marten, red squirrels, badgers, maybe a wildcat."

"I think I saw a wildcat when I was camping," Rose said.

"Did you now? You were lucky; there's not many left."

After that they climbed in silence, steadily up through the trees. Some of the pines looked ancient, and fallen branches lay on the ground covered in moss, fungus and lichen. The smell of wet bark and peat was rich and earthy.

Aileen was close behind Seumas. Rose was having trouble keeping up with the pace. He must have sensed she was falling behind because he stopped. "If you look up, you'll see the squirrel. It always follows me."

Rose saw a flash of russet red.

"And there. See the badger sets." On the bank above the path were a series of holes. "I come out at night to watch them. They're used to me now."

Higher up he stopped by a huge pine. It had an enormous girth and long branches reaching up to the sky, dwarfing the others nearby. "This is my favourite. It's the oldest in the wood. I hope it'll keep going for another hundred years."

Rose put her hand on the bark, feeling the warmth of the tree.

"I thought you might be able to tell Rose something about Torr Uaine," Aileen said.

"Oh aye? What do you want to know?" He looked at Rose. His face was lined and creased but there was a liveliness about him.

"I think one of my ancestors, Catrìona MacGregor, lived there around 1850. I'd like to find out more about her."

"So, you're a MacGregor?" he said, leaning on his stick and looking intently at her now, as if seeing her for the first time.

"Yes."

"They're a strong, independent lot – persecuted in the past. Did you know the name was proscribed for nearly two hundred years? They were hunted down like dogs for a time. My great-grandmother, Mòrag Fraser, lived in Ardlarich, a village near Torr Uaine, when she was a girl. I never met her. She was born around 1833."

"Do you think she'd have known Catrìona?"

"It's likely, everyone would have known everyone around the loch in those days."

"We're connected then, in a way," Rose said. This thought pleased her. She liked his spirit. His earlier prickliness had been justified – after all she'd started asking him questions before they'd been properly introduced.

He smiled for the first time. "It seems so. The first thing you need to know is that the Menzies have owned this land for six hundred years. They lost part of it after the '45, Culloden to you, but they soon appropriated more, common land by foul means. Sport." He spat the word out. "That's what our land is used for, sport for the rich. People could be living here instead. By 1860 most of the ordinary folk had gone. They say it was never as bad as we make out. It was worse." He thumped his stick on the ground, making Rose jump. "Didn't mean to scare you, the wounds run deep. The loss is still tangible. It's in the stones, in the wind, in the earth. This land was full of people; there were babies, children, old ones. It was well worked. Now there's few folk left. It was said my great-grandmother went mad after they were cleared. She walked about the house at night calling out the names of the people that lived in her village. See here?" The trees were beginning to thin out. Ahead of them was a high fence running down the hillside. "The Menzies put this up last month. The Forestry Commission want to plant new pines here, extend the wood further. The Menzies are contesting it. Now it's all held up in the courts. If I was younger and fitter I'd take this down with my bare hands."

"They've been fighting with Seumas for years. They hate him because he's indestructible and they can't get him out," Aileen said.

"Never will. My cottage is on Forestry land but it doesn't stop them trying. I had another run in with Menzies last month. I was taking the path over the tops and I met him and his gamekeeper in their Land Rover. They said the path was closed for essential maintenance. I said I couldn't see any work going on. Fergusson got out and threatened me."

Aileen rolled her eyes. "Robert Menzies never remembers my name. His wife is the same. They live in the west wing of Creag Dhubh and rent out the rest of the house for stalking and grouse shooting. The people who come are mostly men but there are sometimes women. I remember one. She was probably about my age and she was obsessed with killing. I heard her talking once. Said taking a stag gave her more of a thrill than anything."

Rose shuddered. "Torr Uaine is on Menzies land?"

"Aye and it was them that cleared it. There are no records to speak of, only snippets of stories handed down."

"I wonder if they'd talk to me about it."

He laughed. "They'd send you on your way lassie. No time for a MacGregor."

Back at the cottage Seumas invited them in. "Sorry, I'm not used to visitors, you'll have to make do with a stool." The room was painted green and was quite dark, with only one small window overlooking the loch across the road. There was an armchair in front of the fireplace, a wicker chair and a stool. Barney went to sit on the rug in front of the wood burning stove.

While Aileen made a pot of tea Seumas told Rose she should look for the graves of her ancestors at the kirk in Killichonan.

7

CATRÌONA

There was much work to do on the croft. Eòin came to help when he could but he was often busy finishing the new house. Before Catrìona could start the planting there was raking and harrowing to do. That spring was cold and in the mornings the ground was hard with frost.

She was bent over in the field when she heard a call and looked up. It was Daibhidh, who shared a house with his brother, Fionn, at the bottom of the hill.

They'd lived together all their lives. Fionn had been kicked by a horse when he was a young man – the accident damaged his right shoulder and he had no use in that arm. Daibhidh had been planning to marry a local girl at the time but after the accident had decided he couldn't leave his brother.

He was younger than Catrìona but his skin was lined like that of an older man. When he told stories about his childhood his face lit up. His family had come to Perthshire from the Western Isles looking for better land. He said that living on Uist had been a happy time, collecting the kelp from the shore, seeing the otters play on the rocks, watching the fish leap in the surf. "I still miss the sea. One day I'll go back there though I know there's no living to be made."

"*Mhadainn mhath* Catrìona, you're working hard."

She straightened up, her back already sore, though the work was nowhere near done. "Aye, I need to finish this soon or I'll be behind with the planting."

"Came to see if I could help. I have time. Finished mine yesterday." He spoke in short sentences, often missing out words. She was used to it but some people found it odd.

She was about to say no she didn't need help, but looking at the field she realised she would find it impossible to get it done on her own. She also had a lot more weaving to do if she was to finish the shawl in time.

"*Tapadh leat.* I'd be glad of your help."

"Brought my hoe. We can work together."

He began a new row. They worked in silence, concentrating. The energy he put into the work seemed to reinvigorate her.

After a while he stopped, leaning on the hoe. He took a drink of water and then handed her the flask. "Is Eòin settled? It must be strange. Him gone."

"Sometimes at night when the wind is blowing strongly through the roof and Brèagha is restless I feel unsettled. I'm so used to his presence. He would get up first and stoke the fire, put the water on to boil. Still, I'm pleased for him and glad of his decision to marry Seònaid."

"Aye, I know how MacIntyre treated her. Saw him threaten her once. Told him to calm down. He told me to mind my own business."

They worked on. She liked his company, he was quiet, calm and dependable. By the end of the day they'd completed half the field. The sun was beginning to sink at the head of the loch.

"We should stop."

60

"I'll be back tomorrow to finish it off," he said.

She thanked him for his hard work, watching as he walked down the hill. She cleaned the hoe and hung it up and then put the barley on to boil. She'd be glad of a hot meal. She sat on a chair by the fire. Her limbs ached and throbbed, and all she wanted to do was to fall into the box bed and sleep.

That night she missed Donnchadh. He'd been gone ten years. There'd been a cry and she'd come out of the house. He was standing stock still, staring up at Sìdh Chailleann for what seemed like ages, as if he'd seen something, then his legs collapsed under his body. She'd run to him, calling out his name but he'd been still, eyes staring into space, and she knew he was gone. Màiri had come straight away, felt for a pulse and slowly shook her head.

Catrìona still missed him. His big frame and broad shoulders. He'd play the pipe when he was in a good mood; sad songs, fast reels, encouraging her to sing, and had taught Eòin too. He would always tell him, "No man should be without music."

Eòin was still young when his father died, slender and pale skinned. He became quiet and withdrawn. Catrìona had tried her best to comfort him, holding him close, telling him stories in the long winter nights, trying to make him smile again. Over time he seemed to forget his father though he remained fiercely fond of the pipe.

*

Collecting water from the burn Catrìona saw Mairead hanging the washing outside, the baby in a basket nearby.

"How is the wee one?"

"She's well. Màiri's herbs have worked a miracle – I was

61

so worried before, she didn't put on an ounce of weight."

"I'm glad. And the other children?" Catrìona didn't want to mention Jessie in particular. The two of them had agreed to keep the incident with the skull to themselves.

"They're thriving, except for Jessie, who doesn't want to go to school. There was a time when she was up with the lark but that has changed. I've asked her why but she just says she wants to stay at home to help me. I think it's important that she learns about the world."

"It's a pity. She's such a bright girl."

Mairead nodded, pegging the last garment and picking up the basket. "She already knows much more than me. She's stopped dancing too. Can you talk to her, Catrìona? She listens to you."

Catrìona nodded. "Ask her to come to see me."

*

Jessie leant against the side of the loom as Catrìona wove.

"Has the teacher made you wear the skull again?"

"No, Mrs MacGregor. But he does it to other children. It makes me sad. He told Jane to wear it and she cried all day. I was scared to say anything, in case he…"

"I understand."

"I don't want to go to school anymore. I'm twelve now, I could help to earn some money instead. Will you teach me how to weave?"

"A loom is expensive, Jessie."

"I could help you."

She sounded so eager that Catrìona didn't like to say no. "If your parents allow you to leave school I'll give you some lessons."

Jessie skipped around the room, narrowly missing

knocking the pan into the fire. "Yes, yes!"

Catrìona laughed. "Careful." She was happy to see Jessie looking more as she used to. If Mairead and Alasdair agreed, she would make some time to teach the girl the skills of the loom. It might help her to ease the ache of loneliness she'd had since Eòin's marriage.

*

The top of Sìdh Chailleann was covered in dark cloud and the loch was the colour of charcoal. Ripples shredded the reflections of the trees. The wind was swirling around the strath.

Catrìona was on her way to the Black Wood to find lichen for a new batch of dyeing.

As a child she'd been frightened of the place. Her father had taken her by the hand and they'd walked through the wood together, him pointing out the capall-coille and naming the trees, Scots pines, rowan, goat willow, juniper. After a while her fear subsided and now she knew every path, every tree and wildflower.

She walked, feeling the soft ground of moss and pine needles underfoot. It was quiet here, sheltered from the wind, surrounded by the ancient trees, some the width of a man with arms outstretched, outer bark thick like shoe leather, the soft pink beneath. If she put her hand on one she would feel its heartbeat. Picking her way through brambles and over roots, she stopped often to scrape lichen from the bark. She wandered a long way, almost to the edge of the wood where the trees began to thin and give way to Castle Menzies land. Bending to take a piece of white lichen from a rock she heard what sounded like a low groan. Thinking it must be a branch rubbing against another in the wind she carried on with her work. The sound came again. She stopped and listened.

"Somebody help."

She called, "Who's there?" Putting down the basket Catrìona tried to separate a tangle of juniper to get to where the sound had come from. On the other side was a huge tree that had been riven apart, one branch hanging down like a partially severed limb, another on the ground.

The sound came again. "Here."

Ducking under the fallen limb, she saw a man with white hair lying on the ground. She recognised him straight away; it was the laird, Sir John Menzies. A branch was across his chest, pinning him down.

She hurried over and knelt beside him. "Are you in pain, sir?"

"My chest…"

There was a gash on one of his legs, his face was grey and his breathing irregular. Catrìona put her arms around the branch and tried to move it but it was much too heavy. "I must go and fetch help."

"Don't leave me."

She hesitated. He might die if she left, but if she didn't then he certainly would.

"Please."

He looked so desperate that she put her shawl on the ground and sat beside him. Taking a piece of clean cloth from her basket, she tied it as tight as she dared around the cut on his leg to try to stop the bleeding.

"Thank you. Are you Catrìona MacGregor, daughter of Donald MacGregor?"

"Yes sir."

"A good man." He stopped and took a huge inward

gasp as if there wasn't enough air in his lungs.

"Please let me go for help. We must move the branch from your chest."

His face was paler than before. She was terrified he might die while she was there. He gave a sudden gasp of pain and loosened his grip on her arm.

She got up. "I'll be as quick as I can. Hold on until someone comes, please sir."

Picking up the basket and pulling her skirt above her ankles she went as fast as possible through the wood until she came to the entrance to the castle. She hurried up the driveway. There was a large knocker which she picked up and let fall. A maid answered the door and Catrìona told her about the accident. The maid called for a manservant, who said he would send men out immediately to bring the laird home.

They thanked her and she trudged slowly home, tired and disturbed, thinking about what would have happened if she hadn't been there; that he might have died in pain and alone. That night she said a prayer for the laird, asking God to save him.

A day or so later she was coming out of the cottage on her way to start the planting when a man on a bay horse rode up the track. He dipped his hat. "Mrs MacGregor?"

She said that she was and he handed her a note. It was written on official paper in large scrawled lettering. "Please visit the castle at your earliest opportunity." It was signed "John Menzies."

For the second time Catrìona found herself walking up the long winding drive edged with tall elm trees. She wondered what the laird might say to her and whether she'd be told she'd strayed too close to Castle Menzies land.

The maid opened the door. "He's expecting you."

Catrìona was surprised to find that instead of a grand bedroom on an upper floor she was shown into a side room off the hall; it was dark and cold, despite a fire burning in the grate.

The laird was propped up in a bed on large pillows. He lifted a tired hand when she entered. "Mrs MacGregor. Please, sit down."

She went across the room and sat on a chair that had been placed by the bed. "I hope you're recovering, sir?"

"I am, thank you, although there is constriction in my chest, as if the branch was still there."

"Sorry."

"I expect you're wondering why I asked you here? Firstly, I want to thank you for finding me. I would most certainly be dead otherwise." He spoke slowly, with frequent pauses. She tried to answer but he held up his hand. "I'm deeply grateful. There's another reason, which may surprise you. You may remember that your father found my sons?"

In 1815, which was known as the time of the fog, Catrìona had been a young woman. A smartly dressed man had come to the house and asked to speak to her father. Her mother had been anxious. "Is there a difficulty, sir?"

"No madam. I've been sent by the laird to ask for your husband's help."

The laird had four children, three boys and a girl. The two oldest boys had been rowing on the loch; the fog had come down suddenly and they hadn't been able to find their way to the other side. Someone had heard them calling out, then a sharp cry and nothing more. They

66

never returned home. The laird was distraught; the oldest and – it was known, his favourite – child was one of the disappeared. He ordered his men out on a search and soon afterwards they found the damaged upturned boat. There was no sign of the boys.

Catrìona's father was known as Dòmnhall of the Second Sight and had a gift for sensing place. He'd predicted the whereabouts of an old woman who was losing her mind and wandered to the edge of the moor. Another time, he found a baby who'd been abandoned on a hillside.

The laird knew that his sons wouldn't be found alive but he wanted them to have a proper burial so he asked her father to locate the bodies. He'd gone with the messenger and asked for time alone at the loch. When the time was done, he'd told the search party where to find the boys, two hundred yards into the centre of the loch, directly south-east from the jetty. Men were sent with ropes to dive and after several hours located both bodies. They were buried in the grounds of the castle in a specially erected mausoleum and it was said that the laird went there every day to grieve.

Soon after, Catrìona's father received a parcel containing a small, dark wood bowl with a silver rim, engraved "To Donald MacGregor, with gratitude."

"It was a sad time, sir."

"Yes." The laird lowered his voice and she had to lean forward to hear him. "Now I must tell you the truth, for Anthony may come back here. Earlier that day he, Anthony, my youngest and only surviving son, was playing in the boat with his sister Georgina. He had a knife that he took from the kitchen and began to carve a hole in the bottom plank. He told Georgina it was just a game. He filled the hole with earth and covered it with a piece of cloth so it didn't show. She was the youngest and scared of her brother so she did nothing to try to stop him. The boat was damaged when we found it but we thought it had got caught on some rocks."

Catrìona listened, silent and shocked.

He stopped speaking and took a laboured breath before continuing. "Anthony swore Georgina to secrecy. Because she was frightened, she remained silent and lived with that knowledge. That's why she's like she is. Much later she told me the truth. We sent Anthony away to school then. For his own good."

"I'm sorry for you and your wife, sir."

"It was painful for Eliza. She was already sickening but I believed it hastened her end." He put his hand to his chest and grimaced. The light from the lamp fell on his face. He was pale and beads of sweat were forming on his forehead.

"You must not say any more, sir. It's making you ill."

"I needed to unburden myself. Now I can rest. Thank you." He shut his eyes and turned his head away.

She tiptoed out of the room and the maid showed her to the door.

*

The priest gave the news at the kirk. Sir John Menzies had died – his heart had given up, soon after the son returned.

He'd been their laird for almost sixty years, mostly fair and sometimes benevolent to his tenants. Several cottars had been forced to move but he'd planted more trees in the Black Wood and took good care of the boundary walls. The priest spoke about his generosity and compassion and they said prayers for his soul.

"Anthony Menzies is now the new laird. I'm sure we will welcome him to the strath and do our best for him."

Catrìona shifted awkwardly at the mention of the name. Daibhidh, who was sitting next to her, asked if she was comfortable and she said she was. She'd not told anyone the laird's secret, sensing that, although he didn't say, he'd meant it just for her ears – almost as a confession.

The priest was starting his sermon when the kirk door opened. People turned to look, watching as a tall man entered and took his seat at the back. Catrìona caught a glimpse of his face, which was clean-shaven and strong, neither ugly nor handsome, but memorable. There was murmuring, which the priest put a stop to by loudly clearing his throat.

At the end of the service the congregation filed out. The stranger remained at the end of the pew, his head bent forward as if deep in thought. Outside, to the side of the kirk, was a large black horse. Catrìona noticed to her surprise that the reins were trailing in the grass.

On her way home Catrìona went to visit Màiri. Màiri rarely attended the kirk, saying that long ago she'd believed in God but now thought he was the construct of foolish men. Màiri was older than Catrìona but was capable and strong. Catrìona admired the way she managed her house and land with no help from anyone. Her hair was grey, but thick and full and long. She once had a husband who'd disappeared; some people said she'd done away with him, drowned him in the loch in the dead of night. She told no one what had happened, only saying, "He liked climbing, perhaps he went up the mountain and forgot to stop at the top."

Men kept away from Màiri but women were grateful for her advice and treatment for their health problems and always asked her to be present at the birth of their children.

Her medicines were collected from Rannoch Moor. Most people avoided the place; it was wild and inhospitable, with deep and dangerous bogs often concealed by clumps of bog grass. Many men had disappeared while attempting to cross it. Màiri though was unafraid. She could make her way from one end to the other without hesitation, finding the rare and precious flowers and leaves to use for her remedies. Inside the house bunches of plants were strung from the ceiling, and there was an aroma of rosemary and other herbs that Catrìona couldn't place.

Màiri was shredding leaves into a pan. "Herbs for Fionn – he's suffering from bronchitis again."

"We had a service for the laird today."

Màiri snorted. "That old waste of times. Still, I suppose there's some that's worse."

"There was a stranger at the kirk."

She stopped stirring. "Was it somebody interesting?"

"A man. He looked unapproachable. He had a large black horse which had been left free to roam outside the kirk."

Màiri put down the spoon and removed the pot from the fire. She had a thoughtful expression on her face. "Then he may bring trouble. I remember my sister told me when she lived in Glen Lyon that their laird, Montrose, complained the factor was not doing the work well and employed a new one. The man was polite and everyone thought he would be fair in his dealings but the truth was he was vicious. MacGillouvry was his name. The one thing about him that people remembered was that his horse was never tethered."

8

Catrìona walked along the path beside the kirk carrying a bunch of spring flowers, passing the ancient yew tree, grooved and twisted, as old as time. Lifting the latch she pushed open the gate to the churchyard. It was the anniversary of Donnchadh's death. Ten years. In some ways it seemed much longer, a whole lifetime, but in other ways like yesterday. There was a time when she thought she couldn't go on, the crushing feeling when she woke in the morning and realised he wasn't just away in the field.

Despite her fears she'd survived; she'd had to, for Eòin's sake. She was proud of that and, though she missed Donnchadh greatly, some things were better without him, though she would only ever admit that to herself. She'd found a way to manage the work and to earn money as a weaver.

The churchyard was by the loch; the dead had fine views. Leaning on the wall Catrìona looked out across the water, which was still and quiet, feeling the soft earth beneath her feet and the sun on her face. She shed tears remembering the feel of Donnchadh's arm around her and how, when they were young and first married, she wanted him to hold and kiss her every night, so that sometimes he laughed and said, "I'm lucky to have someone who loves me as you do."

She cleaned lichen from the lettering on his grave and

laid the flowers on the grass. Close by was another grave, smaller in size. She averted her eyes until she could bear to look at the inscription. Ealasaid and Anna. Children of Donnchadh and Catrìona MacGregor. Ealasaid died 12 Dec 1828. Anna died 16 Dec 1828.

Ealasaid – eight years old, hair the colour of autumn bracken, purple stains around her mouth from eating blackberries, helping card the wool, running through the heather so light she could bounce on the top of it then suddenly the illness came upon her and she was choking and wheezing. At first they thought it would pass but then she grew paler and one night she breathed her last breath and then Anna was the same. Catrìona had clung onto Anna and prayed and prayed, though she no longer believed in God because after all what was he there for, if not to save her children?

She sank down against the wall, though the ground was wet, remembering those dark times. Other families around the loch had also lost children to the disease. Coffins being walked along the lochside to the kirk were a regular occurrence. Then the sickness had passed and the township returned to a semblance of normal but for Catrìona there was no normality. She no longer wanted Donnchadh to touch her; it would only lead to more children and more sorrow. He was patient with her, though sometimes he would walk the hills and when he returned she could tell he'd been crying.

One night several years later there'd been a huge storm which threatened to destroy their roof. They'd fought to hold onto the heather and make sure that the cow and calf were not too frightened. In the early hours of the morning the wind abated and they went to bed exhausted but elated that they'd saved the house. At that moment she realised they were joined together. He was her friend, the one she'd chosen. She'd reached for him and though he'd been surprised and tentative at first, they'd not forgotten their passion for each other.

Nine months later Eòin was born. She watched over him like a hawk, keeping him close beside her at all times until Donnchadh said, "Eòin needs to come to the field with me now, Catrìona. The danger has passed."

*

On her way home Catrìona heard voices and rounding a bend saw two men coming towards her. One was a head taller than the other. The smaller man looked familiar, someone she hadn't seen for many years. Anthony Menzies. The other was the one she'd seen at the kirk. She carried on, assuming they would walk straight by, but instead they stopped. Mr Menzies raised his hat and said a cheerful, "Good morning. Mrs MacGregor, isn't it? I think I have you to thank for trying to save my father."

She nodded in agreement. "I heard him calling in the Black Wood and ran to fetch help."

"Thank you for your diligence. I'm your new laird, Sir Anthony Menzies. This is Mr MacGillouvry."

She wanted to say, "I know who you are," but stopped herself.

MacGillouvry stared at her. There was something chilling about it, as if he could see right through her, his eyes as dark as his horse. He nodded and said, "Good day." His accent was not one she knew.

Feeling awkward in her old green dress and shawl in front of their fine suits she said, "I'm pleased to meet you.

Good day to you both," then she hurried on.

Anthony Menzies had filled out since she'd last seen him. His face had become fleshy, though his dark curly hair still gave him a childish look. He was now the owner of a castle. If he hadn't made a hole in the boat it would have been his older brother who'd have inherited. No wonder he looked pleased with himself. He would have a good life, all the deer and salmon and wine he could ever want. Still, the castle was huge and isolated. She wouldn't want to live that way. She needed her neighbours, Jessie and the Frasers, Màiri, all the children.

She carried on walking home, past the farm at Ardlarich, stopping to say hello to Sophie MacDonald, who was sweeping the path to her house, rounding the last bend before coming to the turning to Torr Uaine. On the other side of the road was the Hanging Tree, an old oak, very tall, which spread out across the loch and the road. The largest branch was fifteen feet above the ground. Jacobite fighters were hanged from the tree by Cumberland's men after the '45.

Sometimes she let herself stare at it, as if by doing so she could nullify its power; that day she barely glanced at it until a movement caught her attention. A black horse under the tree. It raised its head to look at her for a moment then shook its mane and returned to rooting among the leaves.

*

There were days of sunshine, interspersed with heavy bursts of rain. Wind blew across the hillside at night, whistling through the heather roof. In Catrìona's field neat rows of potato leaves pushed up through the mounds of earth.

Kale was growing thick and full. Eòin and Seònaid settled into the new house. Seònaid made rush mats for the floor and decorated the windowsill with wildflowers.

Eòin came by nearly every day to bring water from the burn. One morning when she'd finished milking Brèagha and was starting the day's baking there was a knock on the door. It was the priest, John Macleod. He'd been at their kirk for several years now. Catrìona tried to like him but found him to be a humourless man whose sermons were too long.

"Good morning, Mrs MacGregor, I hope you're well?"

"Good morning, sir. I am. I hope you are too?"

He nodded in assent. "May I come in? There's something I must discuss with you."

"Certainly."

They spoke in English as he did not speak Gaelic, having been educated in the south.

Catrìona opened the door wider and he followed her in. They sat on the bench under the window. Light shone on the side of his face, highlighting the paleness of his skin.

"As you know we have a new laird." His tone was serious and gloomy.

She nodded, waiting.

"The old laird let many aspects of estate management lapse and there's an urgent need for improvements. MacGillouvry, the new factor, has instructed me to inform you that in order to pay for these, the rents will need to be raised."

His words, though not a complete surprise, were still a shock. For all his friendliness when they met, Anthony Menzies must have already decided that they should pay more. She wondered what man would ask a priest to do his work for them.

"I've already informed the other tenants, Seumas Cameron, Daibhidh MacDonald, Alasdair Fraser and Robert Kennedy."

"And Màiri Ross?"

He coughed and looked aside. "Not yet. In fact, you would do well to tell her."

Catrìona suppressed a brief smile. The priest was scared of Màiri and anyway, she would never let him in her house. "Is there a figure for the increase?"

He coughed again and looked down at his papers. "The rent is to be eight pounds per quarter."

She took a sharp inward breath. An increase of two pounds.

"So much?"

He nodded, lips pressed together. "You may need to make some –" he cleared his throat "– adjustments, but I'm sure you will come to realise it's in your best interests. The factor has assured me that there will be great benefits."

"And do you know what these might be?"

The priest shut the book with a slap and stood up. "At present I'm not at liberty to share that information. Now I must be going. I have many duties to perform this morning."

He tipped his hat and left. She followed him out. As he was walking away Eòin passed him on the track and they nodded at each other.

"Was the priest visiting the house, Mam?"

"Yes son. He wanted to remind me about the funeral of Eliza Stewart next week." She couldn't bear to tell him about the rent increase just yet.

Eòin washed his hands in the pail outside the door. "I've something to tell you."

"Is Seònaid well?"

He nodded, smiling. "She's going to bear a child."

For a moment Catrìona didn't react, disturbed as she was by the priest's words, then she collected herself. "I'm delighted, son."

A child, a new life, so unexpected, its fragility pulled at her heart. On another day she would have welcomed it joyfully. Now, because of the encounter with the priest, she sensed that she and her son were standing on uncertain ground.

"The baby will be born just before Christmas – a wonderful time."

"Yes, it is. Màiri and I will help when the time comes. She'll be pleased to hear the news."

"I'm very happy, Mam. It has come soon but I'm ready. I will work hard to make sure the baby is healthy."

That evening Catrìona stared into the fire and her eyes filled with tears. A baby was wonderful but what a time to be born. So much uncertainty. It seemed as if the new laird was going to bring nothing but trouble to their lives. She wished that she could have done more to save Sir John Menzies.

Early next morning she went to visit Màiri. In rowan trees nearby birds were singing. Màiri was pinning washing on a line, her face cheerful.

"A beautiful morning, Catrìona. I love this time of year."

She waited until Màiri had pegged the last piece of clothing. There were two pieces of news to tell her. She told her about the baby first.

"Eòin will be a good father. There's a strength in him. You gave him that, Catrìona."

"I've some difficult news, too. The priest came to see me yesterday. Our rents are to be increased by two pounds a quarter."

Màiri's expression changed. "They're high enough already. If he wants money all he has to do is to buy less rich food and wine. We've nothing to spare here." She picked up the basket and waved a dismissive hand in the direction of the castle. "Let him try to raise them. He'll be in for a shock."

9

The tenants gathered in Daibhidh's house to discuss the rent increase. Alasdair Fraser, Fionn, Seumas Cameron, Màiri and Catrìona, Robert Kennedy. Eòin was needed at the workshop that day.

They pulled their stools close to the fire. Catrìona looked around at their faces. Their expressions were as grim as she'd ever seen them.

For a while no one spoke.

Alasdair broke the silence. "I could have told you it would come to this, the day that old Menzies died. Changes are happening, usually for the worse."

Daibhidh said, "Can we pay what they're asking?"

"We haven't had an increase in many years so perhaps it's due," Robert Kennedy said.

He was sitting slightly apart from them, as if he was different or better. He wouldn't struggle like some.

Màiri coughed but said nothing.

"Here in Torr Uaine, we pride ourselves that our rents have always been paid in full and on time. Eòin has started earning now so we might manage. There are others who will find it hard," Catrìona said.

Daibhidh said, "Fionn and me have nothing spare. It will mean no money for new shoes when they wear out."

Catrìona glanced down at those he had on. They'd need replacing soon.

"Mairead can't take on any more work, not with the new mouth to feed. That amount no," Alasdair sounded angry as he often was but this time it was with good reason.

Màiri looked up, a reflection of fire in her eyes. "Where's it going to end? There's talk from the north of folk losing their homes. It's a ploy to force us out. Raise the rents high and when we can't pay, get rid of us."

"Och, Mhàiri, you're always thinking the worst of people. Old Menzies was a kind man, it's likely his son will be the same," Robert said.

Màiri looked at him, a strange smile on her face, as if she thought he was the stupidest man on earth. "Maybe he'll be kind to the likes of you, but with folks like me, he'd trample us under his foot before he made a compromise."

Robert Kennedy had more land than most, with three men working for him. The year after Donnchadh had died, he'd come to the house and asked Catrìona to marry him. "Come to live with me. It must be lonely here with only Eòin for company."

For a moment she'd been tempted. He had a large house; instead of one or two rooms he had four. Life would be easier for them. He'd tried hard to persuade her but after a lot of thought she'd realised it was he, not she, who was lonely and what he wanted was someone to work for him. She'd said no. For a while relations between them had been awkward but now they were civil.

There was silence. Smoke curled up from the fire, the fading west sunlight flickering in the window.

Finally Daibhidh said, "We should take a vote on what to do. Those in favour of paying the full rent rise raise their hands."

Two hands went up, those of Robert and Seumas.

81

Seumas said, "I've a new baby on the way, I can't be in trouble with the laird now."

"As the rest of you disagree, what do you propose we do?" Robert said.

"We could put forward a lower figure. We can remind the priest that we work hard to look after the land," Daibhidh said.

"Do not agree to any rise. Once they have their way there'll be no stopping them," Màiri said, putting her hands firmly on her knees.

Catrìona spoke. "I'm undecided. I sympathise with Màiri but maybe Daibhidh is right. If we set a figure of seven pounds per quarter it shows we're willing to compromise, especially if they're going to improve the boundary walls."

There were nods. Màiri muttered, "No good will come of it."

After more debate they agreed to Catrìona's idea and Daibhidh said he would inform the priest.

*

Catrìona tried to forget the trouble – every day she got up with the light and milked Brèagha, then began the day's weaving and baking. Early summer in the strath was clear, colours sharp; dark green of the pines, purple of the hills, blue and white of the sky.

There was no word about their offer. Màiri said she was going to attend kirk, the first time in years.

"I need to know what that fraud of a priest is up to."

The sermon was about obedience – to God and all masters. It was a harsh message, one that the priest usually relished. Often he'd repeat words and phrases for emphasis but that day he appeared distracted. There were only three hymns instead of four and the prayers were short. He was about to start the Lord's Prayer when Màiri stood up. She was sitting near the centre of the kirk, so that although she was small, the priest could see her.

"What's the news about our rents?"

The priest paused, frozen at the lectern. He fixed Màiri with a stern stare. "You are in God's house. This is not the place to discuss such matters, sit down." His disdain for Màiri, whom he saw as a heathen, showed in his voice.

Catrìona stood up beside her friend.

"Mhàiri's right, we need to know, otherwise our future is uncertain."

There were murmurs of agreement. "Aye, we need to know."

He looked at them with disapproval. "We'll discuss the matter in the proper place – outside God's house. You must wait until then."

Màiri planted her feet more firmly in the aisle and said, "I won't sit until you've given me an answer. It's been a month since we made the offer."

Daibhidh came to stand with Màiri and Catrìona. "We must know the truth."

The priest glanced to the side, as if checking a door was open for his retreat. "I will tell you… I've recently heard from MacGillouvry."

"What was his answer?" Màiri said, impatient.

"There are to be no negotiations, the rents will be going up by two pounds a quarter."

There was a clamour of voices. "We cannot pay that. Shame on him."

The priest raised his arms. "Please restrain yourselves."

"What's your role here? Is it not to defend your people, to help protect us from hard times? Or is it to be a traitor?" The words exploded from Màiri's mouth.

The priest's face twisted in anger. "You were never one of my flock."

Catrìona was shocked. "All people are equal in the eyes of God. Isn't that what the Bible says?"

"Please, please, behave yourselves and keep your voices down. You're in God's house. I'm certain that with some judicious saving and a little more work you will find the extra."

Angry voices called out. "I've five children and another on the way, what will happen to us?" "We already work from dawn to dusk on our land, we don't deserve to be treated this way." Babies started crying at the noise around them.

"The decision's not of my making. If you want to appeal then you must find a lawyer. Now please leave." He folded his arms.

Women were trying to calm their children, men were muttering.

Catrìona put her arm on Mairi's and said, "We should go."

The congregation were getting up from the pews. Outside, people were separating and drifting away, unwilling to gather with the priest watching them. Màiri and Catrìona walked away with Eòin and Seònaid in silence.

"As soon as I heard about MacGillouvry I knew trouble was coming. He's a cruel man. The priest is weak and will do his bidding," Màiri said.

Catrìona nodded. "Although it's the new laird who's

the greedy one." Thinking of the hole in the boat. "We can't afford a lawyer, the priest knows that."

"Will they turn us out of our homes?" Seònaid asked.

Eòin put his arm around her. "I'll never let that happen."

"We must all stick together." Catrìona said. "We don't know when it is to change, perhaps not until next year. They'll not get rid of us that easily."

They parted at the fork in the track, Màiri crossed the ford and Eòin and Seònaid went on to their house. Instead of going straight home Catrìona walked to the top of the hill, through the birch and oak wood, the springy heather under her feet and beneath that the peat. Below were the bones of her ancestors, those who'd lived there before – before the English had come and made things impossible. When she emerged from the trees the wind was getting up, dark clouds pushing in from the west. The land was spread out around her, familiar and yet mysterious. Each time she came its mood was different; today there was drama and the clouds looked full and heavy with water. She pulled her shawl closer around her and hurried down before the rain fell.

That night she lay awake, trying to think of a way to increase her earnings. Even if she had the time and energy to weave more cloth there was no guarantee that the shop in Kinloch would be able to sell her shawls. Eòin was on a low wage and Seònaid had no skills other than with the animals. The people helped each other out when times were hard – those that did better shared what they could. When her last cow was struggling to produce enough milk Daibhidh brought her a bowl every day. They all needed some help now but she didn't know whom to ask.

10

ROSE

Killichonan church was set above the road. It was small, of whitewashed stone, with trees on two sides. Rose walked up the steps and tried the handle but the door was locked. The windows were dusty and grey. There was a faded notice in the porch but all she could read were the words, "no longer held here".

The churchyard was lower down, surrounded by a stone wall, close to the loch. The grass looked as if it hadn't been cut for years. Perhaps the relatives, like her, were long gone. Many of the graves were covered in lichen, overlapping, circular growths of grey and white, obscuring the names.

All Rose knew of Catrìona was that she was an older woman in 1850. She found MacIntyres and Frasers, Camerons and MacDonalds. By the wall were two graves set close together. The first was inscribed, "Donnchadh MacGregor 30th May 1840". Next to it was a small stone leaning backwards. Rose knelt down and gently began to clear the lichen away from the lettering. There were two names. "Ealasaid died 12 Dec 1828. Aged 7. Anna died 16 Dec 1828. Aged 4. Children of Donnchadh and Catrìona MacGregor. 'Of such is the Kingdom of Heaven'."

Rose stood up, trying to take in what was there.

She didn't know if Catrìona's husband had been called Donnchadh but the dates seemed to fit. If this was the same Catrìona she'd also lost two daughters. Very young and very close together.

Rose tried to picture Ealasaid and Anna. Perhaps they would be singing, holding hands, giggling at night in bed. She'd always wanted a sister.

"Of such is the Kingdom of Heaven." She didn't understand the exact meaning, although it sounded as if it meant it was the will of God. People must have been more religious then.

She thought of Catrìona coming here to visit each May and then again in December, when there was frost on the grave tops. Two small coffins carried by the loch to the churchyard. People from the villages walking behind in a line with their heads bowed.

She stayed by the graves for a while then walked up to the church. Seumas had told her to look for some writing on the windows. Round the back was a small leaded window. The ground was thick with brambles, but she managed to pull some aside and get a closer look. On the glass were some silvery markings which appeared to be words. She reached up, trying to clean the glass with a tissue but the dirt was ingrained so she went back to the car to get water and a cloth. With the glass clean, she could see two sections of writing. Lowest down were the words – "The people of Torr Uaine stayed here December 1850" and "God find us a home". On the higher part of the window were some words in Gaelic.

Tracing her fingers on the glass, she sensed the fear and desperation of those who had written the messages. December – they were cold, maybe looking for shelter.

Perhaps they had spent several nights there before dispersing. It was a place of separations. What happened to them afterwards appeared to be undocumented.

Rose sat on an old bench at the side of the church. Shutting her eyes she thought she could hear children crying, mothers quieting them, wrapping them tighter in blankets, fathers' voices sharp from the fear of running out of food.

Returning to the car by a different path Rose noticed an old house, hidden in the trees, at the bottom of the burn. She went to investigate. Gorse had grown over the path and she pushed her way through the thorny bushes. It was solidly built with a slate roof. The windows were intact but there was no sign of anyone living there. The door was slightly ajar. She gave it a push and it scraped back across the tiled floor. Straight ahead was a staircase with a door on either side. The left-hand one was open so she went in. The room was surprisingly light, a shaft of sun stretching across the floor. A table and two chairs stood in the centre, as if two people had eaten a last meal there and then disappeared. It had an air of abandonment, smelled of musty wood. She went to the window and looked out. Through a light curtain of trees, she could see the loch.

A wooden bowl sat on the windowsill. Inside was a dead fly and some fragments of coloured ceramics as if someone had broken an object and collected up the pieces. She wondered who the previous occupants had been.

The other downstairs room was empty. At the back was a small kitchen with an old electric cooker and some dusty shelves. There were no plates or cups to be seen. The window was covered in spider's webs. Whoever had lived there had long gone.

She went up the creaky wooden staircase and found a room under the eaves. A small skylight let light into the room. Despite the dust the house felt welcoming, as if the people who'd lived there had been kind. She went back downstairs and sat at the table. She checked her phone – unusually it had a signal.

She called Cal. "How are you?"

"Getting there. I'm good on the crutches now. I've even been doing some cooking. Where are you?"

"I'm in an empty house by Loch Rannoch. I might stay in Scotland a bit longer. I'm glad you're OK."

There was a text from Tòmas. "How's things? Want to come to mine for food later?" She wasn't sure how it was meant. She didn't want a date – her mind was preoccupied with history. Still, it was nice to be asked. She texted back. "What time?"

Tòmas lived on the outskirts of Kinloch, near the river, the last house in a row of cottages. His front garden was full of vegetables, beans growing up a wicker trellis, leeks, onions and carrots. Inside the kitchen had been knocked through so it was part of the living area. He was chopping vegetables.

"I'm making stir fry with tofu, is that OK?" He must have remembered she'd said she was a vegan.

"That's great. Have you lived here long?"

"A few years. I got the job at the kayak centre and moved up from Edinburgh."

"It must be different."

"I don't miss the city. Only my son."

"You've got a son?" She was surprised though she didn't know why – he could easily be a father.

He looked up. "Just one, Iain."

"How old is he?"

"Fourteen. He's at school in Edinburgh. I see him in the holidays. It's hard being separated. Anyway, let's not talk about that right now. What have you been doing?"

"Talking to Seumas, then I went to Killichonan. I found an empty cottage near the burn."

"I know the one. That's where the Stewarts lived. David and Sheila. They left a few years ago. It belongs to the Grant family. They're a bit more liberal than the Menzies."

"It's lovely. The bedroom upstairs is nice and the living room is full of light."

He stopped stirring and looked at her. "Are you thinking of living there?"

"No. I was just interested."

"OK." He turned back to the stove. She fiddled with her glass. She felt embarrassed, as if she was a child and had been caught dreaming of something impossible.

The meal was good. The beans and onions tasted fresh. While they were eating, he told her about his work at the kayak centre. "Some of the young people I teach are naturals, they become part of the kayak as soon as they get in. There's a girl I'm teaching at the moment, Emily, she's only thirteen, she's amazing. I've told her she should think about becoming professional."

"Do you go white water kayaking?"

His face lit up. "I love it. Part of the river is brilliant for it, tricky but not too dangerous."

"I'm not keen on boats. Any kind – I always avoid ferries."

"Why's that?"

He seemed genuinely interested and she almost told

him about her dad but something stopped her.

"I get seasick, I expect that's it."

He asked about her work and she told him about the college and her studio. He didn't ask if she sold her work, as so many people did when they heard she was an artist. He didn't mention money at all.

"I'm working on some drawings at the moment. They may turn into something else – I don't know yet. I've got one on my phone, you can see it if you want."

"Yes."

He came to sit by her on the sofa and she handed him the phone. He looked closely at the image.

"That's really interesting. It's very powerful, I like it. Thanks for showing me."

She was pleased. He got up to put another log on the fire. He was easy to talk to but there was a restlessness about him. She wanted to ask what happened with his son and the mother but it seemed to be a sensitive subject so she didn't.

*

The next day she went back to the empty cottage. She picked some wild flowers from the garden and positioned them in a glass jar on the windowsill. The idea of staying there was growing in her mind.

Tòmas gave her a phone number for the Grants and she called to ask about the cottage. The woman she spoke to was friendly and said it had been on her mind to rent it out again but that she hadn't got around to it. Rose could stay there for a week or two for a nominal rent. The electricity was turned back on and a chimney sweep came. Tòmas brought her a spare mattress and fixed the door so it would shut properly. She thanked him for his help and he said he was glad that someone was going to be staying there. She lit a fire, which drew well.

Aileen gave her a yellow and blue rug and some mugs and cutlery.

"Will you be OK?"

"I'm used to being on my own, and you're not far away. I like it here."

She swept the floors and cleaned the kitchen. Angus lent her an electric hob with two rings and a kettle. It was enough. She stood outside in the sunshine with a mug of tea breathing in the soft air, away from the London traffic fumes and the constant noise.

Opening her sketchbook, she began a drawing. It appeared as an uncurling of something, a stretching out – she held the soft pencil loosely and continued the drawing across several pages, the marks smudging and merging, it was a different way of drawing, like the start of a new story.

In the art gallery and bookshop in Aberfeldy, which was in a renovated watermill, Rose found shelves full of local history. In 1850 two thousand people had lived around the loch. In Killichonan there'd been thirty to forty houses, each with a small croft attached. According to one report the crofters had been comfortable and happy. By 1881 the population of the area around the loch had halved. Now there were fewer than two hundred. She found a small booklet about the Gaelic language. Hills had many names here: Beinn, Càrn, Sgùrr, Binnean, Meall. It had been a Gaelic-speaking area but by the early 1900s there were few speakers of the native language left.

Loch Rannoch was one of the deepest in Scotland. She thought maybe it was full of sorrow at the loss of the inhabitants. She was becoming aware of an older, deeper loss than losing her dad – that of being disconnected from her own history.

Lying in bed, Rose could see the stars through the skylight. Wind rustled in the trees nearby. Late on she heard the sound of an owl. Waking next morning, for a moment she wondered where she was. Above her head, small clouds scudded across a watery blue sky.

11

That evening Rose went out through the back gate, jumping the muddy ditch onto the track that ran around the loch. When she arrived at Aileen's house Lily was sitting on the floor in pyjamas with paper and coloured pencils. Rose had met her once before. She looked like Aileen – thick blonde hair and a fringe.

She beckoned to Rose. "I'm drawing a red squirrel, the one who follows Seumas."

Rose went to look. On the page was a red and orange creature with ears and a bushy tail.

"That's beautiful, it looks just like it."

Lily smiled and squirmed.

Aileen had made supper. "Sorry it's very basic, it's Lily's favourite; pasta and broccoli."

"That sounds perfect."

Lily asked. "Are you living in the empty house?"

"I'm staying there for a short time but my real home is in London. I'll have to go back soon."

"That house is lonely, when I go by there I can hear it crying."

Aileen laughed and said, "She's very fanciful."

"We need our imaginations," Rose said.

After Lily had gone to bed they sat together on the sofa. Aileen yawned. "I'm knackered. Today was hard. There's a big party next week so I had to make all the beds

– twenty-five rooms."

"That's a lot."

"Usually there's another chambermaid but she's off sick at the moment. It was a strange day. There was an odd atmosphere in the house and Menzies and his wife had an argument. I was in the next room. I couldn't hear much at first but then the voices got louder. I heard him say he's instructed the solicitor to get rid of the tenants at Spring Cottage. They're near here so I hope it won't be us next. His wife said, 'Isla liked the MacNabs. What would she say?' He said something like, 'Isla's dead. You can't live your life thinking about her. You need to move on.' All of a sudden there was a loud scream and I thought he'd hit her. I was about to rush in but then I heard him trying to calm her down and it all went quiet."

"It sounds awful. Who's Isla?"

"Their daughter. She always looked unhappy. I bumped into her once when she was coming down the stairs carrying the dog, I could tell she'd been crying. She was really thin, it looked unnatural. I said 'Are you OK?' She stopped and looked at me – she had these really sad eyes. She said, 'No, but you can't help me.' She died a few months after that. I sort of wish I'd tried harder but then there was probably nothing I could have done."

"When was that?"

"About this time last year."

"And he expects her to have moved on already?"

"It's crazy, I know. Anyway, how's the cottage?"

"It's so peaceful after London. I'm reading the diary translations. I really want to know what part the Menzies played in Catrìona's life."

"Have I told you about the archive they've got in the

house? I always hear Menzies boasting about it when he's showing people around. I think it goes back a few hundred years."

"That sounds brilliant. Could I look at it?"

Aileen looked dubious. "The library is always locked. I don't clean in there."

"Maybe there's another way in?"

"There's a door through his study but I'm pretty sure that's locked too. Even if we could get in, I don't think we'd be able to find anything relevant."

"I'd love to look. Sounds like they didn't treat their tenants well."

"I'm sure they didn't but you can't just come here and expect things to change overnight. They're not going to roll over and say, do have your land back, and remember, I need the work." Aileen's expression was one of tired irritation.

"Sorry, I know you've already helped me a lot."

"Look it's OK, I'm just being grumpy. I'll see if I can figure something out."

The sun was going down as Rose walked back. Swallows swooped low over the loch, catching the midges hovering above the water. She thought about going to Perth Library to see if they held any records about Torr Uaine.

Next morning Aileen called. "Good news. I asked Menzies if I should clean the library and he said yes. He's given me the keys. They've gone out so come now. If you go round the back of the house I'll let you in."

Rose parked by the loch and walked up the long drive to the house. Close up it appeared enormous. Walking past the stables she found a small green door. She knocked and after a minute Aileen opened it. She whispered,

"We'll have to be quiet. The butler and cook are around somewhere. If we see them I'll say you're my cousin."

She followed Aileen, who was carrying a bucket of cleaning stuff, down a stone flagged passage with a low ceiling. They climbed a short flight of stairs and then turned into a wide corridor with wooden panelling. Aileen stopped at a large door, put the key in the lock and turned the knob. The room was huge. Two walls were lined with bookshelves from floor to ceiling. There was a long vertical window with a view from the back of the house to the hills.

They surveyed the books.

"It's amazing. There's so much here, where do you want to start?" Aileen said.

Rose noticed a small stepladder in a corner. "I'll start with the top shelves on this wall."

"OK. I'll do the lower ones on this side."

The first shelf was full of plays and novels so Rose moved the stepladder along. At the end of the shelf was a line of box folders. She pulled one out marked "Estate No.15." Inside were plastic sleeves filled with papers, some typed and some hand written in ink. These appeared to be recent reports about numbers of deer and grouse and which years were most successful. The others nearby seemed to be similar and not what she was looking for.

After a while Aileen said, "I can't find anything relevant on the shelves I can reach and I ought to do some cleaning."

There were footsteps in the corridor and a knock on the door. Aileen put her finger to her lips. Rose shut the file and looked around for somewhere to hide. The floor-length curtains at the windows were the only place, so she got behind one.

Aileen opened the door. "Hello."

"I thought I heard voices," a man said.

"I was probably talking to myself, I do it all the time."

He must have come into the room. Rose held her breath. The dust from the files was making her want to sneeze. She held her nose trying to suppress it.

Aileen said, "I'm taking down the files and books, they haven't been dusted for ages."

"That will take some time."

"I know. I better get on."

"I'll leave you to it."

Rose waited until the door had shut and the footsteps moved down the corridor before coming out.

Aileen whispered. "That was close. We've got less than an hour then you'll have to go."

Rose studied the shelves again and noticed an old cardboard box in the far corner. She stood on the top step of the ladder and just managed to reach it. Inside were more papers and files which she flicked through, searching for relevant dates. At the bottom was an old folder marked 1850 – 1860 and inside that was a notebook. She opened it and found what appeared to be records of rent collections. There were place names – Annat, Ardlarich, Killichonan. Right at the back of the book she found Torr Uaine. Underneath was a list of names in black spidery writing. She scanned them, looking for Catrìona. Under "M" was a Donnchadh MacGregor.

"Look at this," she called, forgetting to be quiet.

Aileen came over.

"Rent collections for Torr Uaine. Everything is paid for up to April then in July there's a note against some of them. Not sure exactly what it says, maybe withheld?"

Aileen looked closer. "Could be."

"The next entry's been crossed out, maybe that's when they all got evicted." They looked at each other. "This must be the moment it happened. That is so strange." Rose was holding the book tightly. "Can I borrow this?"

"I'm sorry, Rose, you can't. I'll never be able to put it back. They won't give me the key again for ages."

"OK. I'll take some photos instead." She photographed the relevant pages. At the back of the book she found a folded letter, which she skim read and then took an image of.

She searched a few more folders but the dates weren't relevant. Aileen finished the dusting and said they'd better go, so Rose put everything back on the shelf.

Walking back along the corridor she saw a staircase that she hadn't noticed before. At the top was a large portrait of a man. The face looked familiar. She stopped.

Aileen said, "They'll be back soon."

"Just a sec." Rose ran up the flight of stairs. The brass plaque read. "Sir Anthony Menzies." The face in the painting looked exactly like Cal. She pulled out her mobile and took a photo then ran back down.

"Sorry, it was an interesting painting."

Aileen let her out.

"Thanks, that was really useful," Rose said.

Halfway down the drive she saw a figure coming towards her. The woman was wearing a green jacket. Her hair was dyed blonde. She looked as if she was going to walk past without a word but then she stopped.

"Who are you?" she said.

"I'm Rose, Aileen's cousin." The woman looked blank.

"Your chambermaid."

"Oh yes," she nodded.

"I had to give her a message about a relative who's ill."

"Sorry to hear that." She looked closely at Rose as if trying to work something out. "Are you…? No, of course not, how stupid to think…"

The woman passed her hand across her eyes and swayed slightly.

Rose said, "Are you OK?"

"I'm trying to remember…" She turned abruptly and walked up the track. As Rose was getting in the car a large 4x4 swept past and turned into the estate entrance.

Back at the cottage she looked at the photos of the rent book. At the top of the first page was written, "Property of George Munro, factor." At first the handwriting was clear and upright but after several pages it changed. A new name appeared – "MacGillouvry." In July there were still some rent collections in Torr Uaine; others, including the entry for Donnchadh MacGregor, had a large cross next to the name. After 1850 there were no more entries for the village. She studied the photo of the letter.

> To Anthony Menzies, of Creag Dhubh Castle.
>
> Sir. We are begging you that our rents at Torr Uaine not be increased by such a large sum. We are law-abiding tenants and have always paid our rents on time. We are willing to pay an increase of one pound per quarter. We the undersigned:

There was a list of signatures; the second clearly read,

"Catrìona MacGregor."

Across the top was a note: "Rejected."

They'd been hoping for understanding and acceptance – they'd made a compromise – but instead, they'd been sent away. Her people. Dispersed, scattered, evicted, cleared, cleansed. So many words to describe what happened. All cruel, all hard, all sad.

She went outside and stood looking across the wild overgrown garden to the loch, trying to feel their presence and finding nothing but the wind. She sensed a connection with Catrìona, who was an artist and craftsperson too. What she didn't know was the people's stories, told in their own voices. Those voices were lost.

12

CATRÌONA

21 June was the summer Cèilidh, held each year to celebrate the solstice. Catrìona was outside the house, talking to Màiri and Daibhibh. The sun had risen early and it was a beautiful warm morning.

"Can we afford the extra food and drink? We have so little to celebrate," Catrìona said.

"We should gather and fortify ourselves for the battle ahead," Daibhidh replied.

"It's a chance to tell the neighbours of our troubles. It may soon affect them." Màiri sounded as gloomy as Catrìona had ever heard her.

"They'll be frightened," she said.

"Better they are forewarned." Daibhidh shifted on his heels. "You are on good terms with folk from Killichonan and Ardlarich. News is best coming from you."

"I'd rather not be the one to tell them."

"I can't do it for I would show my rage," Màiri said.

"And I speak awkwardly," said Daibhidh.

Catrìona sighed. "Well then, I suppose it must be me."

Rising early the next day, Catrìona took a large bowl, mixed the oats and butter and added a few drops of precious honey. She flattened the circles on a metal griddle and baked them over the fire. Filling her basket with food she made her way to Daibhidh and Fionn's house, where the Cèilidh was always held. The sun was going down and a breeze was pulling ripples to the surface of the loch, catching the golden light.

Outside Daibhidh was putting out stools in a circle. "It's a fine night. Are you well, Catrìona?"

"I'll be better when I've spoken – the burden of what I have to say is weighing heavily on me."

She took a clean cloth from the basket and spread it over the table, then laid out the honey biscuits and cheese. A bonfire was lit. People were coming down the hill and up the track, young children skipping ahead, women following with their babies. Sophie MacDonald had a twin on each hip. The musicians arrived with their pipes and fiddles. Catrìona was bending to take more food from the basket when she felt someone's arms round her waist. "I'm so happy to see you, Mrs MacGregor."

Catrìona stood up, laughing. "I'm very pleased that you're here, Jessie."

Folk were sitting on every available stool, young ones on the grass at the front, men standing at the back. Fiddle players were tuning up; soon they swung into the first of their tunes. Eòin joined in on his pipe. She watched his fingers moving swift and light up and down and was proud. Sophie stood and began to sing. She had a fine voice. After a while she stopped and beckoned to Catrìona who took her place at the front. Closing her eyes briefly she took a long breath. Her voice rose, filling the air – a song about a boy who sailed the sea. Whenever she sang she felt as if the earth beneath her feet lifted her into another place.

For her next song, *Far am bi mi Fhìn is Ann a bhios mo Dhòchas,* "What I Hope For Is Wherever I Am", she called for Jessie to come to stand with her. Jessie had a sweet, high voice that contrasted beautifully with her own. When the song came to an end there was clapping and some were wiping away tears.

The musicians took a break and folk thronged to the table to fill their plates with food and their mugs with water or whisky. She even had a few sips. It was rare that she drank the spirit but tonight the intensity of what she was feeling made her want it. The liquid warmed her stomach.

Their appetites satisfied they gathered to listen to old Muireach. It was said he was over a hundred years old but no one knew for certain. He remembered everything, even the dark years after the '45 when Cumberland's men came knocking, looking for escapees and survivors of the battle. His two uncles had been killed on the field and another had been captured and executed soon afterwards.

"I'm going to tell you a story about how history changed course."

The children sat cross-legged on the floor at his feet, faces aglow with anticipation.

"My uncle, Alasdair Cameron, was the youngest of five boys. He was handsome, only twenty-one, with dark hair and red lips. When he heard that Cumberland's army were planning to meet the Jacobite at Culloden Moor he had a premonition that things would go badly for the Gaels so he hatched a plan to thwart him. He borrowed a beautiful, blue dress from his sweetheart, one of the chief's daughters, concealing a small, sharp knife in the purse tied around his waist, then he and a small band of loyal Camerons rode for three days to meet with Cumberland's men." At that point Muireach's voice became softer. The children crept nearer. "Cumberland was vain and known to be flattered by the attention of beautiful women. At the camp the soldiers were surprised to see such a lovely woman and readily took him to the duke's tent. When my uncle was introduced, he praised the duke's beauty, although as we know this was a long way from the truth. The duke was seduced by the flattery and ordered his bodyguards out of the tent so he could have his way. But as soon as he tried to kiss the beautiful woman Alasdair pulled the knife from his purse and stabbed the duke in the heart." There was a gasp from the audience, then silence. Old Muireach was gazing at the fire. They waited for him to speak again. "The duke lay dead in his tent and Alasdair escaped before the bodyguards could arrest him. When they discovered he was dead the army was thrown into disarray and knowing they could not win without their leader they retreated back to England." There was another pause and nods and murmurs from the listeners. Then Muireach threw his head back and said louder this time, "And that, my friends, is how it would have been if my uncle Alasdair had not fallen from his horse on the ride to Culloden and broken his neck."

Another loud gasp, then Seumas, the Frasers' boy, asked, "Is that a true story, Mr Cameron?"

Muireach, who was half blind, turned his head towards where the voice had come from. "There is truth and half-truth and there are stories and who knows where the real truth lies."

"A good tale, Muireach," called Daibhidh. "Now let's have more music." The fiddles started tuning up.

Catrìona had heard the story many times before but it never lost its power. No one knew if it was true. Around her people were talking. "How's the new baby?" "When is your youngest starting school?" "Has your cow recovered from the sickness?"

When they'd eaten, Catrìona went to stand in the centre of the circle. Daibhidh called for people to listen. She stood for a moment not wanting to say what she had to say. Màiri nodded at her encouragingly.

"Some of you may have heard that we in Torr Uaine are facing a rent increase, one that we can't afford. So far it's only our township but we wanted to let you know in case the disease is contagious. Our committee has decided that we can't pay the full amount. We have offered the factor a small increase, which has been refused. We can afford no more."

There were cries of "Shame!" "Terrible!"

"We're strong and will stand firm. We hope they'll come to see that we have right on our side."

More murmurs and nodding.

"Until then we're going to enjoy this Cèilidh as we always do and to sing and dance with no fear in our hearts."

There was a cheer and the pipes started up again. The fiddle players joined in, playing slowly at first then faster and faster. Those who could got to their feet to dance. Daibhidh took Catrìona's hand and she was in the centre with everyone, dancing the reels, in and out, crossing arms, small children whirling about between them, before collapsing, laughing and exhausted in a heap. Faces were glowing pink with heat and enjoyment, looking as if their cares were forgotten.

*

Catrìona was worried about Seònaid. At the Ceilidh she'd seemed distant and preoccupied, although she said she felt well. She was a serious young woman and Catrìona thought perhaps the responsibility of being married and worrying about their rents was too hard for her. She offered to teach Seònaid some new cheese-making techniques, which would mean she could spend some time with her.

When Catrìona arrived Seònaid was nowhere to be seen. She called her name but there was no reply from the field. She climbed up the track above the croft knowing that sometimes Seònaid went walking there. It was windy and the clouds were low, brushing the top of the hill. The large outcrop of rock known as A' Chathair was silhouetted against the sky, and a figure stood on it, skirt billowing in the wind. Seònaid. The girl was too far away to call to so Catrìona began to climb towards her. The ground was boggy and she had to jump from hummock to hummock to avoid sinking into pools of water. There was a time when she could have done it easily but now her limbs ached.

The base of the rock jutted out halfway up the hill, like a ledge. She climbed as fast as her breath would allow. When she got closer she called out Seònaid's name.

There was no reply. She called again and Seònaid turned and saw her but all she did was shake her head. To Catrìona's horror, she took a step nearer the edge and looked down. A cry came from her, high and desperate. Catrìona, fearing she would jump, began to climb again, pushing her fingertips into cracks in the rock and clutching at the harsh bog grass, summoning her strength. There was a sapling in a crevasse and she grasped it, hauling herself up the last few feet and onto the rock. Seònaid was standing right by the edge. Catrìona called. "Please, don't jump."

Seònaid hovered. Catrìona held her breath. The girl stepped back and sank down onto the rock, weeping. Catrìona ran to her and knelt down and held her, thanking God that she hadn't gone over the edge.

"Why are you here? What's wrong?" Seònaid raised her eyes to Catrìona but did not speak. She had the look of someone who was tormented.

"Tell me, then I can help you."

"I'm frightened, Catrìona. I don't know what it is to be a mother. What if I don't love my child?"

Catrìona was shocked by her words and tried to think back to how it was for her when Ealasaid was born. So many emotions – excitement, fear, but most of all happiness. "When you see the baby you will, for he belongs to you and Eòin. He is precious."

Seònaid was crying hard. "Is it so easy?"

"It will be well, you'll see. Now we must go down, the rain is coming this way."

Slowly Seònaid got to her feet. They climbed down, Catrìona supporting her. Back at the cottage Catrìona made tea. Seònaid had stopped crying but was very subdued. Catrìona was worried, not understanding why she was so upset and frightened. "You're young but there are many people here to help you with the baby. You won't be alone."

Seònaid looked at Catrìona, her bottom lip trembling. "There's something I must tell you."

*

Catrìona was lying in bed, blankets tucked close around her, thinking about Seònaid. She had talked, shivering by the fire, Catrìona coaxing words from her. Soon after her marriage Seònaid had met Anthony Menzies on the high path, when coming back from visiting her mother. He'd been friendly, offering to help her over the swollen river. When she was safely across he'd held her for too long. She'd pulled away but he caught her arm and told her she must be grateful to him for the life she was living with her new husband. She said she was but it seemed that wasn't enough because he'd tried to kiss her and, when she refused, he became angry. He hit her and threw her to the ground, lifted her dress, tore her underclothes and forced himself upon her. All the time in the telling Seònaid had been shaking and crying, hardly able to get the words out. Catrìona had barely been able to listen, she was so full of emotion.

Finally Seònaid told Catrìona that when she found out she was pregnant she was convinced that the baby belonged to the laird.

Catrìona was shocked to her core by what she'd heard and further disturbed when she discovered that Eòin didn't know. She tried to convince Seònaid to tell him what had happened but the girl was fierce and said she'd rather die than let him know of it, for then he'd be angry and unhappy too and might do something to endanger himself.

Catrìona feared that she was right and agreed not to tell him, as long as Seònaid could persuade herself that the baby belonged to Eòin.

13

Catrìona received a letter, postmarked Nova Scotia. James, Donnchadh's oldest brother, had emigrated there five years earlier. She'd received no word since one telling her he'd arrived and thought that he must have forgotten them.

> *Dear Catrìona*
>
> *I hope this letter finds you and Eòin well. I often think of you and my dear brother. For the first few years we had to work hard clearing forest, of which there are many miles, so we could build our house and farm. The winters are hard here, colder and longer than in Scotland but there is a lot of land for growing. No one bothers us. You would be very welcome to come here. We could help to build you a house nearby.*

She was glad to have news and thought for a second about the offer, especially now as their life in Torr Uaine appeared precarious, but soon dismissed it. She was too old to be starting anew and couldn't imagine leaving Scotland. She showed the letter to Eòin, who said, "I'm pleased to hear from him. I'll write back when I have time."

*

The sun was burning the back of Catrìona's neck as she

stooped to weed the vegetable rows. The strong leaves of the potatoes in the lazy beds reached up for the sun. Turnips and kale were growing well. She fetched water from the burn in the tin bucket – the earth sucked up the liquid thirstily. The shouts and laughter of the Fraser children carried up on the breeze, followed by Mairead's voice calling them in to eat.

She finished weeding and straightened up, trying to ease the ache in her hip. The wind was blowing hair across her face. Pushing the strands away she caught sight of someone coming up the track on a horse. She knew straight away who it was – no one else had such a large beast. She dropped the hoe, wiped her hands on her apron and hurried to the house, arriving just as MacGillouvry was dismounting.

He turned, dipping his hat. "Good morning, Mrs MacGregor. I hope you're well."

She nodded.

"I've come for the rent," he said.

"The previous factor came on the last day of the month."

"I am not he."

"If you'll excuse me."

Her heart was pounding as she went into the house and fumbled in the drawer for her bag. She could feel his presence, outside the door, as if he was blocking out the light. She wished Donnchadh was there for he would have found something to say and given her confidence. She pulled herself up. It was no good delaying the moment. She took out the seven pounds; her hand hovered over the extra pound but they'd agreed and if she gave him that there would be no spare money.

Handing it to him silently, her eyes were lowered. He counted it. "This is not the full amount."

She stood firm though she was quaking. "It's all I can afford." She looked up, meeting his gaze – wanting him to see that she was telling the truth. He stared back at her and did something unexpected; smiled a small smile.

"There will be consequences."

"If you'll excuse me, I need to get back to the field."

He put the money into his sack then took out a rent book and wrote something down, no doubt making a note of the arrears. He remounted then, without tipping his hat, urged the horse down the track. She collapsed against the wall, her legs weak. It wasn't too late, she could run after him, promise to find the rest of the money. She battled with herself; they had made a decision and she must not go against it although she had a sense that they were doomed. He'd seemed pleased, as if a rebellion was what he wanted.

She was about to return to the field then remembered that Seònaid was on her own so she hurried up the hill. The girl was sitting on the milking stool, leaning her head against the cow, although it was not milking time.

"Seònaid."

The girl didn't appear to hear so Catrìona put her hand on her shoulder.

Seònaid turned. "I've done something terrible. I gave him eight pounds. I know we agreed but he followed me into the house and said I must give him the whole amount or there would be trouble. I refused at first but then he came nearer and I was so scared. Oh Catrìona, what will happen now? Eòin will be so disappointed."

Catrìona was fully aware of Eòin's temper, not that he

would ever hurt Seònaid, but he would certainly go after MacGillouvry to protect his wife.

"It's not your fault. He should never have forced himself into the house. We will not tell Eòin."

"But what shall I say about the missing money?"

"I'll replace it."

Seònaid's expression was hopeful. "Will you?"

Catrìona nodded. "Come with me."

She gave Seònaid the extra pound, which meant she had nothing until she could finish her latest shawl. She stayed at the loom for hours, her back aching, eyes straining to see.

At dusk the next day Eòin arrived at her door with a torn shirt and a bloody cut on his cheek. She gasped when she saw him. "What happened?"

"I can't go home looking like this as I will frighten Seònaid."

"Come in and sit down while I heat some water. Have you had an accident?"

He shook his head. "Seònaid was sad last night. I insisted she tell me what was wrong, so she told me about MacGillouvry forcing his way into the house. In her condition anything could have happened. I was angry so I waited for him on the track to his house in Kinloch."

"What happened?"

"I asked him for the time, then as he was looking for his watch I pulled him from that horse."

Catrìona gasped. "That was foolhardy."

"He's a liar. He said that she invited him in. She would never do that."

"This isn't a game." She had soaked a cloth in warm water and was gently dabbing away the blood. He winced

113

as she touched the cut. "MacGillouvry is not a man to be messed with. Times are troubled enough, we can't afford to make them worse."

"He deserved it."

"And if he calls the constables, they will believe him, not you."

"I'm praying he won't."

"It's sad that you were without a father for much of your young life, he could have shown you what was right. He never used violence."

"I remember once when we were out on the hill catching rabbits, I caught my ankle in a deep hole and twisted it when I fell. It was the most painful thing I've known. He sat with me and gently held it with his big hands. He didn't tell me to stop crying. After a while it stopped hurting and we carried on walking. It felt like a miracle."

"He was a patient man and a good father."

The blood was gone leaving a narrow cut along the cheekbone. It would bruise.

"What will you tell Seònaid?"

"That a piece of wood broke away as I was sawing."

*

The tenants held firm. Each had their own story to tell about MacGillouvry.

Catrìona told Daibhidh what had happened to her.

"I was scared and tempted to pay but I stood my ground. Now I am worried about Eòin and fear he may be heading for trouble again. After Donnchadh died he misbehaved at school and was beaten for it."

Daibhidh nodded. "I remember."

"This time it's more serious." She told him about the fight with MacGillouvry.

"It's understandable that Eòin would be angry. We must hope that MacGillouvry won't send the constables. I've news too, Catrìona. I did what we agreed. Did not pay the full amount. Then MacGillouvry told me that the laird wants to put my field together with two others to make one big farm. Someone from the south wants it. He can make more money like that. If we agree we can have six months at the old rent." He sighed and looked at his hands, lined and scored from years of hard work. Catrìona waited for him to continue. "What shall I do, Catrìona? I love this place as much as the island now."

He looked up and she saw the tears in his eyes, which made her want to weep too.

"Where will we go? To Pitlochry, Perth, Edinburgh? It is not the strath."

She reached across and put her hand over his. "I don't want you to leave. This is your home."

"We don't own the land, we've no power and Fionn is more and more often unwell."

She didn't know what else to say so they sat in silence and watched as the rain moved across the hillside.

That night she dreamed of her mother. Her mam was always busy in the house and scolded Catrìona if she daydreamed or played too long outside with the other girls but sometimes when she was in a good temper, she would sit with her by the fire and tell her a tale of a *brùinidh*. In the dream Catrìona was sitting on her mam's knee listening to one of her mother's stories. The *brùinidh* was helping around the house, whistling and sweeping up. Catrìona made the mistake of giving the *brùinidh* a name, for she wanted it to be her friend, but the *brùinidh* hated this more than anything and changed shape into a tall thin, grey hooded creature with skeletal hands that reached out, plucked her from her mother's knee and stole her away.

She woke from the dream disturbed, fearing being taken away from her community, from Daibhidh, from Eòin, from Màiri and all the others.

14

ROSE

Rose climbed the hill behind Torr Uaine, wanting to explore the land where Catrìona had lived and worked. The stone ruins were on a gentle slope but the land behind rose more steeply. She headed for the top of a chain of hills around the north of the loch. It was a warm day with a breeze and the cloud was high enough to keep from the tops. Taking her paints and pencils, she set off on the well-marked track past the village. Soon the view opened out, layer upon layer of hills, stretching into the distance. The colours were intense in the morning light, deep umber, soft green, the pinkish glow of the heather. As she climbed the path grew steeper and more indistinct until it ran out altogether and she was following animal tracks. Above was an outcrop of rock, jutting out from the slope of the hill.

By the time she reached it she was breathing heavily and feeling the pull on her leg muscles, which were unused to hills. The last part was steep and to pull herself up onto the slab she had to cling onto clumps of bog grass. Below the shapes and colours of the land were laid out before her like an aerial map. The loch and the river glinted silver.

She sat on a rock and took out her paints and paper and began a painting of the stony outlines of Torr Uaine, with Schiehallion and the Black Wood in the background.

Mixing the paint and brushing it across the damp paper, watching it bleed into the colour next to it, was an absorbing process. When it was finished, she saw that she'd managed to capture something of the wild beauty of the landscape but at the same time she had an awareness of the privilege that was hers – to just admire the view. Catrìona must have had to work extremely hard and rely on good weather to produce the food she needed in order to survive there. The painting dried quickly in the breeze and she returned it to her backpack.

Taking a different path down Rose headed for the pale line of the track, jumping across boggy holes and pushing through patches of heather. Underneath a solitary rowan tree was a large brown shape. She stopped. A bird. One wing was spread open as if it was broken. The wingspan was huge. Her heart was beating fast. Thinking it could be a golden eagle she knelt beside it and touched the feathers. The bird didn't stir. She lifted the wing so she could see the head – the eye was glazed over and the beak was open. She looked for signs of injury but apart from the wing it appeared undamaged. Maybe it had died a natural death, but why here and not higher, where its nest must be?

She took a photo of the bird and then one of the wider landscape, so she'd remember where it was, then sat on a rock close by, glancing occasionally at the beautiful feathers, imagining it flying overhead, wondering how it had died. She hated to see dead creatures. Once while she was waiting at a bus stop in London a pigeon had been knocked by a lorry; she'd cried out loudly and the pigeon tried to get away but the lorry started forward and crushed it in front of her. For days she couldn't erase the image from her mind.

Back at the cottage she called Tòmas and told him about the bird.

"How tragic. They're such amazing birds. There's a wildlife crime officer, John Wilkie, based in Killin. Hang on, I'll get his number. Did you photograph it?"

"Yes, I know exactly where it is."

"They'll pick it up and try to find out what killed it. Is it on the Creag Dhubh estate?"

"I don't know where the boundaries are."

"Let me know what happens."

She called the number. It rang for a long time. When someone picked up the line was crackly. She told him what she'd seen.

"I'll check it out. It will have to be tomorrow, I'm miles away."

"Can I go with you?"

"It's not usual procedure."

"I can show you the exact spot."

"OK then. I'll pick you up."

Next morning there was a knock on the door. The man was about her age, not dressed in uniform. He showed his ID. "I'm John."

They shook hands.

"I thought this cottage was uninhabited."

"I'm staying here for a short time. I was camping but it didn't work out so this is the next best thing."

"Not much of a holiday finding dead birds."

"I wasn't looking. I was painting."

She showed him the photo.

"That's definitely an eagle. We have two pairs in the area. Let's go and find out what we can."

It was a bumpy ride but it didn't take long to reach

the top of the track. She pointed to the rowan tree. "Over there."

They made their way up but when they got to the spot the bird had gone.

"It was here yesterday. Look, that's where it was lying." She pointed to a depression in the grass.

He pulled on a pair of surgical gloves and knelt down. "There are traces of something here, and look, a couple of feathers. I'll take them to the lab for tests but unfortunately it rained overnight so I doubt if we'll get anything from them."

"I thought I saw an eagle when I was camping here, high above the crag. It's really sad."

"Aye. It may have died a natural death but we do see a fair amount of wildlife crime. It's hard to get prosecutions though."

"Whose land is it?"

"This belongs to the Menzies."

He gave her a lift back to the cottage.

"Thanks for notifying us. I'll let you know about any developments."

*

The following day Rose was woken by a sharp knock on the door. Thinking it might be John with some news she pulled on her jeans and ran down the stairs. She unlocked the door and looked out but there was no one there. On the doorstep was a crow, large and black. The eye socket was empty. Around its neck was a piece of string with a note. She bent down. Her hands were shaking. It read, "Go back to England."

Rose stood rooted to the ground unable to move. The

eyeless bird stared back at her. She looked around, fearful, as if someone might be hiding in the trees, watching, but could see no one. Maybe someone had seen her with John and realised what she was doing.

This place that she'd gone so readily to explore was more complex than she could have imagined. She suddenly felt very alone. The cottage was remote, sometimes with no phone signal. She was digging around and some people didn't like it.

She went back in the house and found an old piece of cloth and a pair of scissors. She cut off the note then gently wrapped the bird and took it to the end of the garden where she covered it with leaves.

She wanted to call someone to hear a familiar voice. Her mum would worry, Aileen would be busy getting Lily to school and Tòmas would be at work. She phoned Cal.

He sounded cheerful. "Hi, how's the digging going?"

"Umm OK. I'm finding out stuff." She was about to tell him about the eagle and the dead crow but he started talking. "I'm playing the guitar again and Frank called, you know from my last band, said did I fancy getting together, trying out a few new songs. I said yes."

"That's great, Cal." Not wanting to depress him she told him about the cottage. "It's right by the loch. I've met some nice people here."

Still on edge after the call, Rose got in the car and drove to Kinloch. The sun was threading through the trees – another beautiful day. It was a strange country, swinging from being alien, frightening, unfathomable, to being beautiful and accessible and back again.

She went to the pub to say hello to Angus.

"I'm glad to see you. How's the cottage? Anything

you need?"

"It's good. I've got everything."

"Aye it's a lovely spot there. They should renovate it properly so someone could live in it."

"How's Shona?"

"She's well. Visiting the grandchildren in Pitlochry this week."

After the pub she went to the shop. The owner's daughter, Blair, who was shy and didn't meet Rose's eye, was serving. She was wearing a wooden brooch in the form of an exotic bird.

"I love your brooch," Rose said.

"Thanks." Blair looked up. "I made it in art class."

"It's beautiful. Do you like art?"

"I want to be an artist but Mum says it doesn't pay the bills."

"People said that to me too but I kept doing it and I'm still here. The thing is when you're creative you find ways to survive, that's an art in itself."

"Can you tell her that? If she heard it from someone else she might let me go to college."

"I will, next time I see her."

Not wanting to spend the evening alone Rose called Tòmas and invited him for a meal. After they'd eaten, they went down to the water side and sat on the beach. The sun was sinking at the end of the loch and the water was still. In the centre was a family of ducks. The bare rock of Schiehallion was catching the orange glow of the sun.

She told him about the crow and showed him the note. He studied it. "I don't recognise the handwriting but then I don't think I've ever seen Fergusson's. It's nasty, sorry. There is some antagonism towards the English but by leaving a dead bird it sounds as if whoever it is is trying to scare you away. If he thinks you know about the eagle and he's responsible for its death he could be warning you off. It's terrible that raptors are being killed to protect the grouse moors. Eagles survive extraordinary hardships, harsh cold and winter storms; they're amazing, but they can't survive guns and poisoning. It's big business here, the estates make a fair amount of money. They wouldn't be able to keep the land without it."

"I don't want to go yet. I haven't read the whole diary. I'm sure there's more to find out."

He looked at her, sympathetic. "You don't have to go. If you don't feel safe you can stay at mine for a bit – you could have Iain's room. He's not coming back for another three weeks."

She felt a tug of attraction, as if she'd physically shifted towards him, which she hadn't. She thought about it for a moment. His cottage was small so they'd be very close. She liked him and knew he was trying to help but friendships with men always seemed difficult; there were so many possibilities for misunderstanding.

"Thanks," she said, "I think it was just a warning though, not a real threat. I need to stay at the cottage, close to the family graves. And besides, I've started doing some art there now."

He nodded, and she thought she saw a flash of disappointment cross his face, but he just said, "I understand. The room is there if you change your mind."

She stood up, a bit awkward, as if she'd been asking for help and then rejected it when it was offered.

"Thanks for coming over, Tòmas. I feel a lot better now."

The next day an email from Bridget arrived with more translation.

July
Jessie is a good pupil. She has woven several inches of
the shawl. It is well done. She will make a weaver.
No word from the priest about our offer. We are praying
they will accept. The summer is warm. I must water
the crops often. Daibhidh helps me every day.
Màiri has picked meadowsweet on Rannoch Moor for
Mairead.

There were notes about dye colours for a new shawl and at the end a poem.

Chreag Riabhach

A chreag riabhach air a breacadh le crotal
Buidhe is geal is uaine
A chreag riabhach le beAnnag de dh' fheamainn
dhonn dhorca

The Grey Rock
The grey rock is spotted with lichens
Yellow, white and green
The grey rock wears a dark brown shawl of seaweed.

Rose had read about Rannoch Moor. It was the largest wild place left in Europe, remote and dangerous to cross, full of hidden bogs and sudden mists. Maybe if she climbed the hills west of Torr Uaine there would be a view.

The weather was fine, a few clouds in the west, that was all. Soon she was looking back down on the village, the Black Wood, Creag Dubh Lodge. In the distance she could see the ruins of Castle Menzies. As she walked energy coursed through her body. She took a track going west and, after climbing the last rocky part of the hill, looked down. A huge expanse of moorland stretched away from her as far as the eye could see. Ahead, a mountain rose up straight from the peaty bog. The moor was covered in heather and lochans, small and large lakes of water with islands. A person would get disorientated there and forget which way they were heading. She sat on a rock and admired the magnificent view.

The wind was picking up and she could feel a cool dampness on her skin. The clouds, previously on the horizon, had moved closer. She shivered, zipped up her orange jacket and began walking down to the track. The wind increased and turning she saw that the cloud was almost upon her. She walked as fast as she could but soon it enveloped her. The mist was like a substance thicker than water, attaching itself to her clothes and making her hair lank and heavy. She could only see a few metres ahead. The compass indicated that she was heading south-east which was the right direction, but after what seemed like ages, she still hadn't reached the track. The terrain grew boggier and she stumbled over a rock and slipped, falling into a hidden pool. She pulled herself out cursing. Her feet and calves were soaked through. She was getting very tired but knew she had to keep going and began jumping from hummock to hummock, trying not to slip.

The ground began dipping steeply and fearful she might be heading for a cliff edge she stopped. Her breathing was fast and she was becoming panicky. She sat on a rock. Pulling out the map and compass she figured she must have gone too far west. "You're not far from the track, it's close, you just need to calm down and you'll find it."

She shut her eyes and began to cry.

When she looked up the mist was beginning to thin around her. A gap appeared. She was looking out across an expanse of moorland, which was now a lot closer.

At that moment she heard a high-pitched cry, like that of a bird of prey. She listened. The cry came again, this time sounding like a human voice. Scanning the moor she noticed a flash of turquoise, visible against the muted colours of the landscape and wished she had binoculars. The voice called again. She thought she heard the word "help." Someone was on the moor.

She began making her way down, carefully picking a path through the scattering of rocks and grassy hummocks. Every so often there was a deep drop. As she got closer she could see the person was lying against a rock on the other side of a lochan. A flash of blonde hair. Menzies' wife.

"Are you OK?" Rose called.

"I've twisted my ankle."

"Hang on, I'm coming." She skirted the water's edge. "It's lucky I heard you; I was about to climb back up. I'm Rose."

"Marianne. I've seen you at the lodge."

"Yes." She wasn't going to explain.

Marianne's coat was torn and covered in mud.

"What happened?"

"I was running down the hill."

"Running? Here?"

The boot was undone, exposing her ankle, which seemed to be at a strange angle.

"It might be broken. Can you move it?"

"A bit but I don't think I could put any weight on it."

Rose searched in her pocket for the phone.

Marianne said, "There's no signal."

She was right and it was getting late. It would be dark soon.

"I'll have to go back up. There was a signal when I was on the hill."

"Don't leave me please." Marianne grabbed her arm. "There are strange creatures on the moor."

"Only deer, surely."

"I hate being on my own in the dark. Help me to climb."

"It won't work if you can't put weight on it."

"I want to try."

She looked very scared and Rose couldn't say no. "OK. But it will hurt."

Rose put her arm under Marianne's. Marianne pushed herself up from the rock and swayed, holding her foot just above the ground. Luckily she was shorter than Rose and fairly light.

"This is going to be really difficult," Rose said.

Marianne put her arm around Rose's waist, Rose took a step and Marianne hopped. She groaned and swore, the words sounding strange coming from her mouth.

"How is it?"

Marianne gritted her teeth. "I can do it."

They took another step, Rose aiming for the easiest ground. They were making slow progress until they reached the part where the hill grew steeper.

Marianne collapsed on a hummock, crying. "I'll never get up there. You'll have to go on your own." She sounded desperate.

"I'll be quick. What's your husband's number?"

"Don't call him."

"Why? He'll be worried."

"He'll be angry."

"I have to."

Rose put the number in her phone and began the ascent. Further up the hill she checked the phone again and saw there was a one bar signal. She called the number and Menzies answered straight away. "Hello?"

"Mr Menzies. My name's Rose. I'm with your wife – she's had an accident on the moor."

There was a sharp exclamation.

"Is she injured?"

"She's broken her ankle, I think. She can't walk."

"Tell me where you are. I'll call mountain rescue."

Rose did her best to explain. "I'll stay with her until you get here."

"Thank you. It may be an hour or so."

She climbed back down, exhausted and cold. All she really wanted to do was have a hot bath and go to bed.

Marianne was sitting huddled where Rose had left her. She was shivering.

"They're coming. Are you cold?"

She nodded. "I thought I might die by myself. I don't know why I live here. I must be mad."

"Don't say that."

"Why? That's what Robert says."

"Were you running away from him?"

"We argued about Isla, my daughter." Her teeth were chattering. "We're always arguing now. I couldn't stand any more of it. I ran out. He didn't follow me."

The words were out of her mouth before Rose could stop them. "How old was your daughter when she died?"

Marianne looked at Rose with surprise.

"She was almost twenty-one. Very young."

Rose put her hand on Marianne's. It was stone cold. "I'm sorry."

"She had an eating disorder. She never thought she looked right, even though she was beautiful. We tried everything to get her to eat, being kind, being pushy, nothing worked. No one else knew what to do. I thought she was asleep – I remember smiling and thinking how lovely she looked. The dog was with her in the gazebo. She didn't answer when I called her name. She'd taken paracetamol. That's what killed her."

After that Marianne stopped talking. They huddled together for warmth. The sky was going dark and there was no trace of the earlier fog. An hour passed. Then another thirty minutes. Suddenly, above the noise of the wind and the occasional call of a buzzard they heard a shout.

Rose called back and flashed the light on her phone. "Down here." Her voice was croaky and small.

On the brow of the hill were the silhouettes of five people. As they came closer Rose could see that four were in mountain rescue suits. Robert was with them.

He hurried towards them. "Marianne, are you OK?" He knelt down and put his arms around her.

"Yes, thanks to Rose."

He turned. "Thank you for finding her."

One of the rescuers checked Marianne, taking her pulse and blood pressure, and after asking some questions, gave her painkillers. They wrapped her in a silver blanket then very carefully lifted her onto the stretcher. She was trying not to make a fuss but her mouth was gripped tight shut.

Another of the rescuers spoke to Rose. "What about

you?" He looked sympathetic.

"I'm OK, just cold."

They began to climb back up, keeping the stretcher horizontal. Rose followed. There were two vehicles. The first took Robert and Marianne. Rose said goodbye. Marianne, who looked calmer now, took her hand. "Thank you."

The second Land Rover took Rose and the other rescuers. They dropped her back at the cottage. "You did a great job. She didn't have a lot of strength left."

She pulled off her wet clothes and ran a bath. There was never much hot water but she lay in what there was trying to warm her frozen legs. She thought about Marianne running away from her husband. It was lucky that she'd spotted her. Now she knew why the moor held such a mythic power. It was wild and once there you could easily get lost.

In the early hours she dreamed the crow was flying towards her. It was speaking – trying to tell her something urgent – but she couldn't understand the language. All of a sudden it dropped to the ground and lay with its eyeless socket staring up to the sky.

15

Two days later Rose found a note in the hallway.

"I've got something for you. Call me. Marianne."

Dumping the bag of shopping she dialled the number.

Marianne answered and said, "Meet me by the old boathouse near the Black Wood in half an hour."

Rose drove along the loch and parked. Not long after, a dark blue car pulled up. Marianne got out. Her ankle was in plaster and she had crutches for support.

"It's broken, they patched me up. Luckily I've got an automatic car so I can still drive."

They were standing by the wall of the abandoned boathouse. The doors were rotting and falling from their hinges.

"What did you want to tell me?"

"I heard someone reported finding a dead eagle on the estate. Was that you?"

Rose hesitated but they already knew it was her. "I found one up near the crags."

"Did you know we've been investigated before? They didn't find anything that time. Fergusson is clever." Marianne looked around. Even though they were a long way from the lodge she seemed nervous. "I was sleeping in the back room the other night which is where I go when I want peace. I went to the bathroom in the middle of the night and looked out the window. There was a bright moon and I saw a figure in the field. I'm sure it was Fergusson – you can't mistake his size. He was carrying something heavy – struggling not to drop it. He went round the back of the barn and I waited for a while but he didn't reappear so I went back to bed."

"When was it?"

"A few nights ago. I must have been half asleep but when I heard about the eagle from Robert, I remembered it."

"So the evidence is there somewhere."

"Possibly."

"I need to tell John Wilkie."

"I know but please don't say where you got the information."

"Why are you telling me this?"

Marianne shifted her weight on the crutches, looking across the loch. "Eagles are special."

"If your husband finds out you've told me, what will happen?"

"I don't know. All I do know is that everything is already wrong."

Rose drove to Tòmas's house. He was in the garden tying bean shoots onto bamboo poles.

"I know what happened to the eagle."

He stopped what he was doing. "What?"

"It's hidden behind a barn on the Creag Dhubh estate. Marianne saw Fergusson carrying a heavy weight in the middle of the night, it must have been that."

"We'd better call Wilkie."

"By the time he gets there it might be too late. We should go and look."

Pippa, Tòmas's dog, appeared and dropped a stick in

front of Rose, her tail wagging. Rose picked it up and threw it across the grass.

"I'm playing at the pub tonight."

"We could go after that."

He laughed. "I see you've made up your mind. OK, I'll come and pick you up later. I'll bring a spade."

He arrived just before midnight. "Are you sure about this?"

"I'm sure."

They drove along the track leading to the back of the estate. There was cloud but behind that a gibbous moon. They reached the top of the field and could see the barn, about thirty metres away, standing alone. Dotted around the walls of the field were the white shapes of sheep. Barbed wire ran across the top of the wall.

"I'll go first," Rose said. Tòmas held the torch so she could see. She put her toe between the stones and holding a wooden post pulled herself up.

"Wait, I'll pull the wire down."

Balancing on top, Rose swung her leg where the wire was lower and jumped down. He passed her the spade and did the same, and they began walking across the grass. They reached the barn and Tòmas shone the torch on the ground. It was churned with boot prints and covered in sheep droppings. Rose went round to the other side. By the barn wall was a patch of turf in a rough circle.

"This must be it." She took the spade began to dig. The turf came away easily. She dumped spadefuls to the side and soon black plastic appeared. Carefully removing the rest of the earth they lifted the bag from the hole. Inside was the eagle, its head lolling on its breast.

Tòmas took a large sack from his backpack and put the

whole thing inside. "We better get going."

"We should put the turf back."

Just then a dog barked. Once, twice. They looked at each other. Rose's heart was beginning to pound. "Let's go."

They began walking as fast as they could across the field. The dog barked again and another joined in. Rose looked back and saw a light go on inside one of the side buildings.

"Run," she said.

They ran. Someone shouted "Stop!"

Rose didn't look back. The barking was getting louder. "Keep going," Tòmas panted. They reached the wall and threw the bag and spade over.

She began to climb. Her jacket caught in the barbed wire and for a few moments they struggled to free it. There was a ripping sound as she jumped.

Tòmas was climbing. Rose could see the figure of a man, dogs running ahead.

"Hurry," she said.

He jumped down and they began to run. The track was dark and Rose stumbled on loose stones, only just managing to keep her feet. She could hear Tòmas close behind. The noise of the dogs was fading. They made it back to the car, Tòmas started the engine and pulled off the verge.

Rose was panting. "That was close."

"Yes," he said, through gritted teeth. "We'll go to mine, it's safer."

She didn't argue.

They put the eagle in the shed. "I'll take it to Wilkie tomorrow. I hope the evidence hasn't been destroyed,"

Rose said.

"That was probably Fergusson chasing us. He's going to be raging."

Safe inside the house Rose realised how shaken up she was, and how muddy.

"That could have been dangerous. Are you OK? Do you want a shower?" he said.

She looked at him. "I could do with a hug."

For a moment he looked confused, then he opened his arms.

It felt strange. She hadn't had much physical intimacy for a while but there was something familiar about the contact. They held each other for a few moments. Then she stepped away and said, "I'd love a shower."

Once she was done, they settled on the sofa, needing to unwind after the drama. He'd given her a pair of his trousers, as hers were covered in mud. It felt strange pulling them on, as if she'd crossed an invisible line separating them.

"Will he know who it was, do you think?"

"He'll have a good guess. You might find another crow on your doorstep."

"Let's hope there's enough evidence to prosecute him. Marianne said they'd tried before and failed."

"That often happens. The landowners have a lot of power and the laws are often weighted to suit them. You care a lot, don't you?" His eyes rested on hers for a moment.

"I love wildlife. Every creature is precious, especially now that so many species are under threat." She liked being with someone who appreciated nature and wildness.

After they'd chatted for a while longer, she said she needed to sleep.

Iain's room was small with a single bed. On the wall were several selfies of a smiling father and son, out on the hills in all weathers. The window looked out to the side of the cottage up a wooded river valley. She could hear the sound of water rushing over stones.

She thought about Tòmas. She sensed they'd become closer; she'd been conscious of wanting to kiss him but had held back in case it was too soon.

In the morning he made toast and coffee. Pippa seemed pleased that she was there, wagging her tail and putting her head on Rose's knee.

He laughed. "She likes you."

When they'd finished, he washed the dishes. Suddenly he turned from the sink. "Rose?"

"Yes?"

"I wondered if you'd think about staying a while longer in Scotland. To be with me."

He was standing holding the drying cloth. He looked both awkward and determined.

She was taken by surprise. "Oh." There was the sound of the wind in the trees behind the house, rain scratched against the glass.

"I like you a lot," he said.

She was embarrassed and looked down, fiddled with the silver ring on her middle finger.

"I like you too, Tòmas." She found it easy being with him. He was different to most men, much quieter, more diffident. There was a sensitivity – almost a musicality – about him. "We've only known each other for a short time."

"Long enough."

"I live in London though. Everything is there. My

136

work, my friends." She paused. "And I'm no good at relationships."

He shrugged. "Who is?"

She said, "Let me take the eagle to Wilkie. We can talk again later."

As she drove with the eagle in the boot to Killin she thought about Tòmas. She was drawn to him and he sounded as if he meant it when he'd asked her to stay there. Almost as soon as she began to consider it, Sam, her last boyfriend, came to her mind. The particular day he'd told her that his girlfriend was back.

"I'm sorry I didn't tell you about her before. I wasn't sure she was going to come home."

"So you thought you'd keep your options open and sleep with me?"

"It wasn't like that, Rose."

"That's exactly what it was like."

She'd got up off the brown leather sofa – she still remembered the smell of it; it made her feel slightly sick – and picked up her bag, wanting to say something that would have an effect on him but unable to think of anything. She'd run down the stairs and out of the door, then walked all the way home crying, not caring who saw her.

*

Wilkie's office was located in a small police station in Killin. It was a one-storey pebble dash building set back from the road. She parked in the small car park and went to the door.

He came to meet her in reception. "Hello again, Rose. How are you? What have you been up to?"

She wasn't sure up until then how much a part of the police he was but as he had an office there, she assumed he must be. She was a bit worried about telling him how they'd found the eagle, in case they could be prosecuted for trespassing. In the end she did tell him, although not about Marianne.

He went out to the car with her and took the bag from the boot. "I'll take this to the lab later. There's a waiting list so it'll be a while before we get any results but I'll tell them it's important. Thank you for trying to help."

Later she called Tòmas. "I've thought about what you said. I need to know what happened with your wife. Why you're not together."

There was silence on the other end of the line.

"I want to understand."

She heard a sigh. "We hadn't planned to have children, we hadn't even discussed it, but Cara got pregnant soon after we met. When Iain was born I adored him. Cara was earning more money than me so I did most of the childcare. I carried him around in a papoose, took him to nursery. I loved it. Then she lost her job. The law firm she worked for were sued. For a while she was out of work so I got a job teaching music and she took over the childcare. Iain was about six then. I hated the school I taught in but it paid the mortgage on the flat. When she got another job, she insisted we send him to private school. I didn't want to. We argued about it but she was determined. In the end she asked me to leave. I stayed nearby in Edinburgh but I was more and more unhappy."

There was another silence.

"I'm still listening."

"The doctor offered me drugs but I said I preferred

crying. In the end I had to get away to survive. I need to be close to nature, it's what keeps me grounded, my connection with the mountains, the water that comes down from the mountains. I saw the job advertised at the kayak centre. The rest you know."

"And Iain?"

"He comes here in the holidays. I go there some weekends. We're close. That will never change. I figured out I had to save myself if I was going to be any use to him as a dad. We go walking when he's here, miles and miles, working our way through the Munros of Perthshire. It's what we love."

"Thanks for telling me. Sorry I had to ask."

"That's OK. I understand."

She thought of the first time she'd seen him, brown curly hair falling over his face. It had become familiar, the slight Roman nose, high cheekbones, hazel eyes, straight dark eyebrows.

Maybe this time it would work.

16

CATRÌONA

Catrìona was getting ready for bed when there was loud knocking on the door and Eòin came rushing in.

"Sorry, Mam. It's Seònaid, she's sick. Can you come?"

"What's wrong?"

"She has pains and is bleeding."

Catrìona pulled a shawl around her nightdress. Outside the moon was shining, helping to show the way up the track.

Seònaid was curled up on the bed, holding her stomach. There was a large patch of blood on her underclothes. Catrìona knelt next to her.

"How bad is the pain?"

"It's terrible," she whispered.

She felt Seònaid's forehead, which had a film of sweat on it. "You have a fever. We must fetch Màiri. Eòin, go at once."

When he'd gone Catrìona fetched a bowl of water and set it on the fire. "I'll help to wash you and Màiri will give you medicine to help with the pain."

"I think I'm losing the baby."

"Try to stay calm," Catrìona said, attempting to hide her own fear.

Màiri arrived. She pulled a stool next to the bed and

took Seònaid's hand, talking to her in a low voice, one of experience. She turned to Eòin, who was standing at the end of the bed. "I must examine her. Let us have privacy."

Eòin stepped outside. Màiri felt Seònaid's stomach and then gently inside.

"Everything seems normal. It may just be that the baby was shifting around. You need to rest. No carrying or pulling heavy weights."

She took two small bottles from the pocket in her apron, mixed a few drops from each in a mug and gave it to Seònaid. "Drink this. It's a bitter taste but it will help with the pain."

Seònaid sat up and took the mug. Her face looked pale in the candlelight. When she'd drunk the medicine, they helped her to change into clean underclothes, and Catrìona bundled up the stained garment to take home to wash.

Outside Eòin was pacing.

Catrìona said, "She needs to rest. Please try not to worry; it will make matters worse."

"It's that man MacGillouvry. Everything was fine before he came here and terrified her."

Catrìona nodded, knowing that the truth was much worse. "He's making things hard for us but we must stand up to him."

"I don't know, Mam. I love this land as much as you do but Seònaid and I, we're young."

"What are you saying?"

He looked down, unable to meet her eyes. "I'm thinking about accepting Uncle James's offer."

It was like a stab. Such a big step and he hadn't mentioned it to her. "I didn't know."

"I've only just thought it. Seònaid is unhappy and there's trouble here. It might be best."

"We'll talk some more when Seònaid is better. Don't make any big decisions at this difficult time." He looked so anxious that her heart went out to him. "Go back inside now and look after her. I'll call by in the morning."

Catrìona stumbled down the hill, the moon still bright, chilled to think of him leaving, going far away. They belonged here. This was MacGregor land. She was born a MacGregor and married a MacGregor. Their roots ran deep in the strath, flowing with the burn, up to the crag, down under Creag Dhubh Rock. The colour of the heather, pale blue sky after a storm, white water tumbling over rocks in the burn, peat-coloured water in the deep pools, tasting pure and sweet, cool in the throat on a summer's day – all these wonders were theirs.

Her spirit resided there, an old woman's spirit now, no longer that tall, young girl who worked hard and walked for miles, only tired at night as she climbed into the wooden box bed, covering herself in the blankets next to her husband.

That night she lay awake, an image of Eòin and Seònaid before her, holding a tiny baby, their boat tossing from side to side on the high seas.

*

An idea was forming in Catrìona's mind. She knew the truth about the new laird. He was greedy – had killed so he could inherit, and he was cruel and violent too.

She could go to the castle, tell him what she knew – not about Seònaid, for she wanted to protect the girl from further shame, but about the boat. With this knowledge she could persuade him to change his mind about the rents. He might deny it but his reputation would be tarnished if the word got around.

Taking a short cut to the castle, by way of the hill, she could see the two grey spires spiking skywards, piercing the green canopy like needles. Clouds rolled in over the top of the mountains from the west, chased by a following wind. Her heart beat loudly in her chest as she walked, legs were stiff and awkward as if they had no blood running through them. What she was planning might be dangerous, even illegal. She tried to sing to calm herself – but all she could hear was Donnchadh's voice in her head, "What are you doing? Where are you going, Catrìona?" Round and round, like a fateful chorus, until she cried out, "I must do something." Looking around in case someone had heard, but there was only an eagle wheeling in the sky high over the crag, waiting for a shivering young rabbit to run from the burrow.

The tall lime trees towered over her, swaying and bowing in the wind. Her footsteps on the stones would wake the dead. The black door was soon in front of her. She reached up. The bell jangled inside the house and after a minute, she heard footsteps and the door swung open. A different maid stood there.

"Good day, my name is Mrs MacGregor. I'm a tenant at Torr Uaine. I wish to speak with the laird."

"Do you have an appointment?"

"Sorry, no."

"He doesn't see visitors unannounced. I can pass on a message if you wish." The maid was holding the door tightly as if she wanted Catrìona gone.

Catrìona stood her ground. "It's very important."

A male voice in the hallway said something which Catrìona didn't catch. The maid said, "It's a Mrs MacGregor, sir. She wants to speak with you."

The door opened wider; the laird stood in front of her.

"Good morning, Mrs MacGregor. How can I help you?"

"I'm sorry to bother you, sir, but might I have a few minutes of your time?"

"What is it concerning?"

"It's a private matter."

"You'd better come in then. Annie, see to the fires."

She stepped into the hallway, noticing for the first time a large portrait which she thought must be his father as a younger man. Her legs felt weak after the long walk but he did not offer her a seat. Now that she was there, words failed her.

"You said it was important." His tone was impatient. He folded his arms across the protruding stomach.

"We've been told that our rents are to be raised."

"That's correct."

"It's a very large increase, sir."

He shrugged. "They haven't been raised for a number of years. There are things happening beyond this valley that you may not be aware of, in the wider world, in London, that affect us here. Costs are rising. There is more to be made from sporting estates, deer stalking, so those who remain must pay."

His tone was arrogant, as if he thought she was a stupid old woman.

She took a deep breath. It was time. "I know what you did."

"I beg your pardon?"

"Your father told me. When I came to see him here, before he died."

"I didn't know that you were here." The patronising tone was replaced by one that was harder.

The ancestor stared down at her with an expression she couldn't read. The hallway was cold and dark. The stair walls were hung with swords and guns.

"He told me it was you who caused the accident that killed your brothers."

At first he looked surprised, then amused. "I don't know to what you're referring."

"You carved a hole in the bottom of the boat and your brothers drowned. You knew they were going out in it that day."

He looked at her with an expression of intense dislike. "You've no right to come here, accusing me of such a heinous crime. What happened was a tragic accident – tragic – my poor brothers, but I had nothing to do with it. That was the ramblings of a sick man."

"Your father was a good man of sound mind. He looked after his tenants. Will you not do the same?"

He put his hand up. "Enough of your insults! Keep these accusations to yourself. If you repeat this slanderous story, I'll have you locked up. Now leave."

He advanced towards her. She wanted to say more but he grasped her arm and pulled her towards the door.

"Go, and be grateful I haven't sent for the constables."

Outside the door, he gave her a push. She lost her balance and fell down the steps, landing on her shoulder, crying out. Behind her the door slammed. She lay on the cold ground, her head spinning, her right arm throbbing. She attempted to pull herself up and failed. Tried again and again with her left arm and finally managed to stand. She began to walk, slowly, down the drive. Beyond the castle gates she leant against a tree. She shut her eyes and wept, knowing she'd failed.

The walk home was long. She collapsed onto a chair by the fire holding her arm, hoping that no bones were broken. She was a stupid old woman, thinking she had power over the laird. He had no moral bone in his body. All he needed to do was to deny her accusation – after all, who would believe her? They would just think she was one of those crazy MacGregors.

That night she couldn't sleep. Her arm throbbed and no position was comfortable. In the morning she went to Màiri's cottage and told her everything, from the time of being summoned to see the old laird, to what had happened the day before.

Màiri gently moved Catrìona's arm up and down.

"Nothing's broken, it's badly bruised and the pain may take time to go. It's best to keep using it, but don't do heavy work. That was a brave thing you did. Foolish, but brave. Now we know that the new laird is worse than the last. That's no surprise."

"I should never have gone. I've probably done more harm than good."

"You did what you thought was right. The only other person who knows the truth is the sister?"

"Yes, but she's hidden away and no one would believe her either. The chance is gone."

17

Catrìona was seated in the pew. Around her the congregation was restless; there was shifting and occasional muttering. The priest began the sermon and when he spoke the words, "God sees everything that man does," he appeared to be looking straight at her. After the service he followed them outside. "I've a message from the factor. You must all pay the increased rents. A Writ of Removal will be issued to those who refuse."

There was uproar. The priest stood, his arms folded, in front of the door.

"I'm merely the messenger – giving you a warning. You know what you must do."

"If we pay the increase we will starve," someone cried out.

He raised his hands. "Cease. I've told you what will happen, now please all go home."

With that he turned away and went back inside the kirk.

Catrìona saw Daibhidh and Robert standing under the yew tree. From their stance she could tell they were arguing.

"We made an agreement. Now you say you've paid the full amount. You can afford it but what about the rest of us?" Daibhidh said. Turning to Catrìona, "He's saving his own skin and his hearth."

"Is it true?" Catrìona said.

"Aye and if you'd agreed to marry me you could have lived the rest of your life on this land."

She stared at him. He was betraying them and taunting her.

"You have money and your own way of doing things but I'd never have thought treachery was one of them."

He looked at her and for a moment she thought he'd apologise but instead he said, "You will see in the future that I'm right."

Daibhidh took her arm. "Come, Catrìona. He's not worth our anger. We have more important things to think about."

*

The tenants gathered at their meeting place at the foot of Rannoch Rock, a large outcrop of granite close to the loch road. Throughout the afternoon more and more tenants arrived, and others came from Killichonan and Ardlarich. The word had got out about the Writs. "You're our neighbours. We want to help."

Catrìona addressed them. She was growing used to speaking in public. "We'll need to keep watch on the rock for the constables. They could arrive any time. We must prevent them from entering the village and giving us the writs."

Voices called out. "Put me down for the first morning." "I'll do from midday to sundown." "My boys will do an afternoon."

Jessie said she wanted to be part of it. Mairead said no but Jessie managed to persuade her by saying she would join Catrìona.

Catrìona made a list of names and times. "Our signal will be the whistle. If you see anyone who looks like the sheriff and his constables, blow a long note three times as loud as you can."

The mood amongst the tenants was positive. They were ready to stand up to the laird. A few said they didn't want to be involved – Robert, of course, and the MacKays, whose son sent them money from Edinburgh and who said they didn't want any trouble.

Catrìona took her turn as lookout. September was beautiful; sunlight appearing to flow across the loch and once or twice, in the early morning, the first hovering of mist.

Nothing happened. People passing on their way to Kinloch waved and called, asking if she was well, and she waved back saying she was. Two people approached on a horse but it was only a farmer and his son from the other side of the loch.

Màiri came to relieve her, bringing food for them both.

"It could be days, weeks. Maybe it won't happen at all."

"That spy of a priest has probably told them that we've set up watch here. He'll wait until we run out of patience then tell the constables," Màiri said.

"I wish he'd do what a priest should and help his congregation."

Màiri laughed grimly. "He's in the pocket of the laird."

A week passed and still nothing happened. When she was at home Catrìona kept her ears turned towards the Rock, listening out for the call of the whistle. In the township people tried to go about their business – plan for next year's crops, tend to the chickens and the cows, but every time they passed each other there would be an exchange – "Any news?" and a shaking of the head, "Not yet."

Every day she touched the walls of her house and admired the strong timbers of the roof. She'd been born there. Her father had died before she met Donnchadh, and her mother a year later. The laird had allowed Catrìona to stay on and it solved the problem of where they were to live when they got married. Her mother had worked hard, looking after Catrìona and her older brother and sister. There had been many happy days as a child. Catrìona's favourite time was at the winning of the peats in spring, when all the families gathered at the moor to cut their fuel for the year. Her father was strong, wielding the iron with vigour, and working together with Alasdair Fraser they cut many peats. At dinnertime there would be bread and, as a special treat, berry jam. She and Mam would stack the soft peats into little feet, three peats at the side and one across the top. After they were dry, she would help Mam bring them back home on the barrow. When they were well stacked her mother began making the supper, chopping the kale and mixing in the barley. She hung the pan from the pot chain with her long strong fingers, the glow from the fire lighting her handsome face. She too would have fought to defend her home.

Catrìona was again on the Rock. Jessie climbed up to join her. "It's not your turn, Jessie, you don't have to be here."

"I like being away from my brothers. We're always fighting. They have more fun than me, they go out with da in the field, I always have to do the washing; it's such hard work."

"Things will be different when you grow up. You'll

have a husband to help you."

Jessie laughed and blushed. "I can't imagine a husband but if I have one, he'll have to be very handsome."

Out of the corner of her eye Catrìona saw something moving. Dark shapes on the road in the distance; she couldn't make out who or what, but was certain it was more than two people. Jessie caught her expression and turned to look behind her. "Are they coming?"

"Aye, perhaps. Keep watching. We'll wait a little longer."

The shapes came nearer. Catrìona was as sure as she could be that this was them. There were at least three horses with riders, possibly more.

Catrìona blew her whistle. Long bursts of a single note. Three, then she stopped, then another three. She said, "Run, Jessie, run fast. We need everyone here."

Soon tenants were streaming over the brow of the hill and down the track. Daibhidh, the Frasers, the MacDonalds, Eòin, Màiri, the Stewarts, the MacDougalls, the Camerons. Catrìona climbed down to join them. By the time the horses approached there were thirty or so tenants, forming a barrier across the track.

There were four riders. The sheriff, MacGillouvry and two constables. Three dismounted, the sheriff stayed on his horse.

"It's a fine day for a visit," Màiri called out. Others joined in. "Aye, welcome to Torr Uaine. Come to take tea with us, have you?"

MacGillouvry spoke first. "You've refused to pay the full rents. We gave you time to reconsider and yet no one here has given me the correct amount. We've no option but to issue you with Writs of Removal."

"Not true. You could reconsider," Catrìona called out.

The sheriff spoke. "This is now a matter for the law. Your laird has a right to raise rents when he sees fit. I would advise you to comply."

The constables stood awkwardly, looking as if they didn't want to be there.

MacGillouvry was holding a sheet of paper and began to read out names.

"Mhàiri Ross."

Màiri laughed and stepped forward straight away. MacGillouvry handed her the piece of paper. She took it and immediately tore it into shreds. A cheer went up.

He looked as if he might explode. "That will do you no favours, Mrs Ross."

"I want none from you."

He looked at his paper. Everyone waited. "Catrìona MacGregor."

She stepped forward, energy running through her veins. "Take it back to your laird and tell him this is our land."

Another cheer. "That's right. None of us want them." As more names were read out some dropped theirs into the mud, others tore them into little pieces first.

"Eòin MacGregor." Eòin stepped forward and Catrìona felt trepidation flutter in her stomach.

MacGillouvry stepped towards him, his expression turning colder. "You're the one that pulled me from my horse."

"I had good reason."

"The sheriff is here – I'll have you arrested."

"There were no witnesses.' Eòin looked around. "Anyone here see me do it?"

The tenants were shaking their heads. Catrìona wished her son had less bravado. Her husband had been the same but he'd also known when he needed to play their game.

Eòin made as if to accept the writ, then when it was handed to him, he dropped it in the mud and put his heel hard on it.

"Arrest this man, sheriff."

The sheriff looked reluctant. The constables stepped forward, waiting for the order, but the sheriff shook his head. "No. We'll stick to the business in hand. Is anyone going to accept these papers?"

There were jeers from the crowd. "On your way, we'll no be leaving here."

The sheriff instructed MacGillouvry and the constables to remount their horses and return to Kinloch.

"This is not the end – you still have to obey the law," MacGillouvry said, as he swung the horse around.

As they rode away the tenants cheered.

18

ROSE

When the wind was in a certain direction, Rose had to climb the hill behind the house to get a signal on her phone. There was a new email from Bridget so she downloaded the file and then hurried back to the cottage to read it.

"This part of the journal seems very personal and hard to read. I believe I have the correct translation. Any queries let me know. B."

There were entries about the cow and notes on how the crops were faring. Then something different.

Seònaid is in distress. She told me a secret and I am not to tell a soul, especially Eòin. I keep the diary hidden. Soon after they were married, she met the laird on the high path. At first he was friendly then he tried to kiss her. When she refused him he forced her to the ground and pulled up her dress. She is sad and shamed. I wish I could help her.

Rose read the words again. Her hands shook. "Pulled up her dress" could only mean one thing. Seònaid – newly married and happy. The laird owned the land and believed he owned her too. Rape. Sexual assault. Happiness removed.

She heard a faint scratching noise somewhere at the back of the cottage and went to the kitchen. Outside the branch of a hawthorn tree, spiky and misshapen, was scraping against the window. She locked both the doors and returned to the email.

Seònaid is pregnant. She is unhappy and frightened. She thinks it may not be Eòin's baby and that she will not love the child.

The fact that it was almost a hundred and seventy years later didn't lessen the horror of it. Seònaid was Rose's relative; her great-great-great grandmother. Her family. Perhaps the rape had remained a secret for all this time, although anyone who spoke Gaelic and read the diary after Catrìona had died would have known.

The last page of the document began with another note from Bridget.

"This is the translation of a letter from Canada that was attached to the back of the diary."

Now he is born I know the truth in my belly. Donald belongs to AM. I will love him but he will always be a reminder of the humiliation of my body. Eòin does not suspect. Let no one find this letter.
Seònaid.

The words hung on the page. Donald was a Menzies. Rose studied the family tree pinned to the wall. The ink line stretched from Donald down to her. He was her great-great-grandfather. There was roaring in her head, as if she was trapped in a gorge with a flood wave approaching. Through semen, through blood, through violence, she, Rose, was descended from the Menzies.

That night it was hot under the eaves. She tried to open the skylight but it was jammed shut. Her skin prickled.

She thought of Seònaid on the high path, Menzies on top of her. Bile rested halfway between her gut and throat.

The reason the portrait in the lodge had reminded her of Cal was because they were descended from Anthony Menzies. It wasn't just her imagination or some wild coincidence. She wondered if Donald had ever suspected, sensed a withholding of his mother's love, given instead to the next child, if there was one, or if the secret had remained between the two women. Hidden in the Gaelic language was the truth.

She slept badly and woke late. When Tòmas called and asked her to come to the pub to see them playing, she said, "Sorry, I can't."

There was a pause. "Is something wrong?"

"I'm preoccupied with the diaries." That much was the truth. "I'll see you tomorrow."

The day felt long, interminable. She began drawing, making angry marks with hard-tipped pencils, page after page, ripping them from her sketch book and screwing them up. When she was done, she knew what to do. Use her anger – turn it around, like a sharpened spade dug into peat.

*

The butler answered the door.

"I'm Rose MacGregor. Can I speak to Robert Menzies?"

He looked her up and down. "Is he expecting you?"

"No."

"What's it regarding?"

"I've something to tell him."

"I'll see if he can spare a few minutes." He opened the door wider and she walked straight in, after all she had a right to be there. The hall was large, marble floors and wood panelling. Antlers adorned the walls, arranged in order of size, the largest at the top. Each had a bronze plaque. On either side of the stairs were glass cabinets on plinths filled with stuffed creatures, a striped cat baring its teeth, a large black bird with a red beak.

The butler disappeared through a side door. Rose waited. A grandfather clock ticked loudly. After a few moments Menzies appeared, followed by the butler. Now she could see him in the light. He was tall, wearing a tweed jacket and spats, and he had dark hair, silvering at the sides. The eyes and eyebrows gave him the look of Cal. It was unnerving.

"Rose, isn't it? You found my wife. I'm grateful."

"I need to talk to you."

He looked surprised. "I've got very little time today."

"It's important."

"Well, if you insist." He gestured to a door. "We'll go in there. It's alright, Malcolm." The butler nodded and left.

The room was decorated in viridian green. Elegant chairs were arranged around a long table. A chandelier hung at each end. Huge windows gave a view of a wide lawn leading down to the loch.

He pulled out a chair. "Have a seat."

She perched on the edge. He remained standing. A sense of entitlement, like a waft of perfume, emanated from him. His green tweed jacket was flecked with orange and she noticed that his hand, resting on the mantelpiece, had perfectly manicured nails.

She hadn't planned what to say. Rage suffered and churned in her gut. She needed answers.

"As you know, my name is Rose. Rose MacGregor.

What you don't know is that my ancestors lived in Torr Uaine, until they were cleared."

He raised his arms, exasperated. "What's this about? That was a long time ago. It has nothing to do with now."

"In 1850, Eòin MacGregor, my great-great-great-grandfather, married a young woman called Seònaid. Anthony Menzies was the laird."

He nodded. "Yes. He was exemplary. He did excellent work on the estate, planted trees, looked after the farms."

She shook her head. "No." Pushing a fist into her palm. "He was a criminal. He attacked and raped Seònaid."

He stared at her for a few seconds as if unable to comprehend what she'd said. "That's a lie."

"It's the truth. Seònaid had a baby boy. It was his. The baby was my great, great grandfather, Donald. So you see – we're related."

There was silence. In the distance she could hear a mower. The sun streamed in the windows throwing diagonal patterns across the polished wooden floor.

"You're crazy. How dare you come here making up malicious stories?"

"Check the DNA, we can easily prove it."

"I'll do no such thing. Now go."

He moved towards her and she stood, afraid he might strike her, ready to defend herself.

"You stole the land from the people who lived on it, the MacGregors and other families. You raped women, and now you kill birds and animals."

"Get out, before…"

She went towards the door then stopped. "I have a brother. He looks like you. He could be your son."

"What's that to me?"

"I heard you lost your daughter. I'm sorry."

His face twisted in rage; and underneath, something else. "What do you know of pain?"

"My father died when I was a child. It was the hardest thing."

His face softened. For a moment it was almost as if they were on an equal footing, not enemies on either side of a deep divide.

Then he remembered. "Now you must leave."

"Your time here is running out; the hunting estates will soon be gone."

"Get out."

*

Walking down to the car, Rose's body was numb and cold. She hadn't achieved anything by telling him. The Menzies were immune, untouchable, and they'd dismiss her allegation as if she was nothing more than an irritating midge.

On the way back she stopped at the track to Torr Uaine. It had begun to rain. She climbed up past the village to the high path where she imagined Seònaid had met Anthony Menzies. The rain was relentless. At the top she looked out across the landscape, wishing the water would wash the pain away, down the track, into the burn, into the deep loch. She wondered what Seònaid looked like, whether she'd been fair-haired or dark, short or tall, like Rose; if she had ever forgiven herself for what happened that day. Rose knew that those who are abused often blame themselves, as she herself sometimes did for her father's disappearance.

She was soaked through but didn't care, she hated Robert Menzies – for a few moments he'd seemed human but really he was cruel, like his policies on the estate, the hierarchy of ownership, the arrogance of those who thought they were better than the other poorer creatures of the world.

Rose walked amongst the stones. The burn was swollen and rushing over the rocks. She sat under the holly tree at the place where she'd found the shuttle, trying to make sense of what she now knew. Wondering if the mix of genes and confusion of where her ancestors belonged had had a strange effect on her family.

As she was getting up her foot knocked against something protruding from the ground, where the soil had been washed away. She bent down to investigate, digging into the earth with her fingers. A shape emerged; round, with a rim of metal. She pulled it out of the soil and held it. The wood was dark and rotting and the metal tarnished. It could be silver. It looked as if there were words engraved in the metal though she could not read them.

She cupped the bowl in her hands. Maybe it was Catrìona's. Perhaps she'd lived there, in the house with the holly tree. Rose put her palm on the wall, feeling the hands that had lifted the stones, the sounds that would have been heard at the time – the cries and laughter, the stories and songs.

19

CATRÌONA

Catrìona was at the loom, Jessie beside her at the spinning wheel. She could make an even thread and was progressing with her weaving lessons. Catrìona was humming as she passed the shuttle from side to side.

"What's the song called?" Jessie said.

"I don't know yet. It's a new one. I'll keep humming and we'll see what happens."

After a while she began to sing.

The strath is where I belong
My spirit is here still
From crag to moor
From burn to wood
I'll never leave and go.

My people are like roots of trees
Our bones are down below
We love the Earth
It keeps us strong
We'll never leave and go.

Jessie was singing with her, the spinning wheel whirring. "It's beautiful. Will you write it down so we don't forget it?"

A shadow appeared at the door. Without a word MacGillouvry bent his head and came in. Jessie jumped up, knocking over the wheel.

Catrìona stood and said, "You've no right to enter my house."

"But madam, the door was open. I must inform you that the laird has made a complaint against you. You and your son are troublemakers. If I had my way you'd be arrested but instead you're free. If you think this is freedom, living in a dung heap."

"This is my home, sir, my community. We have each other; we have our music and our songs."

"Soon there will be less reason for your singing. I'm here to give you the Writ of Removal."

He took a piece of paper from his bag and put it on the table, thumping his fist on it so it stayed flat. The house, which a moment before had been a place of joy, was filled with his malign interference.

"I do not want it."

"But now you have it. You've been given twenty-eight days to remove yourself and your goods. Plenty of time."

Catrìona drew herself up. Anger was singing in her blood. "Please leave my house and don't return."

"You went too far in going to see the laird. Yours is first, and then that of your son and daughter-in-law. Good day."

Jessie had righted the spinning wheel but she was sitting on the stool crying. "Will you have to go? What will happen to your house and to Brèagha?"

Catrìona went to her. "I'm not going anywhere. He believes he's in charge but there are many of us and we'll say no to him." She tried to sound convincing though now she had the writ she knew the threat was real. "Go home to your mother, Jessie. Tell her that MacGillouvry is out and about."

When Jessie had gone she picked up the paper and studied it. Some of the language was hard to understand but she knew what it meant.

The Tenant is ordered to Flit and Remove themselves, Bairns, Family, servants, subtenants, Cottars and dependants, Cattle, Goods, and gear and to leave the same void, redd and patent, that the Pursuer or others in his name may then enter thereto and peacably possess, occupy and enjoy the same in time coming.

She stood by the door, staring out across the field to the mountains beyond, wondering if it was the end. Her body was weak, the energy draining away. She had an urge to walk down to the graveyard, lie next to her husband and go to sleep as he'd done. She looked around her home. A dung heap, MacGillouvry had called it. The woven mats on the earth, the small objects that she'd collected over the years and kept on the window sill. It was her griddle and pots, her mugs and plates, kept clean and neatly hung and stacked. Her box bed that she'd shared with Donnchadh, precious and cherished. Màiri was across the burn, Jessie down the hill, Eòin and Seònaid and their growing baby nearby. She could feel the connection with the earth, knew the energy she'd poured into nurturing the land and her community, who in return had held her close, so that she'd been able to face anything, even Donnchadh's death and the years when the harvest did badly.

They had no law to protect them, there was only the

strength they could muster. The mood in the township was hopeless and morbid. People stood outside their houses talking. "Aye, we have ours too, only a month to remove everything. What will we do?" Children were distressed, babies keeping their parents awake at night.

The priest put a notice on the kirk informing them that they could claim compensation for the loss of their animals; the money could go towards their passage to Pictou Island or Nova Scotia. None wanted to be uprooted.

Catrìona met with Daibhidh, Eòin and Màiri. "We have a few weeks left. We must think of something," she said.

"But what?" Daibhidh asked.

"I'll write to my cousin in Pitlochry for advice and to see if he can help. If necessary, organise another look out. They don't have enough constables to get rid of us all," Catrìona said.

"Anyone who tries to come into my house to evict me will suffer. I may be small but I'm a match for any man when my temper is raised," Màiri said.

Meanwhile the tenants carried on their daily business, needing to work to eat. One day Eòin called by on his way home. "I've seen the MacNabs packing their goods in the cart along with the children."

"I'm not surprised, son. They have six now – they're too frightened of what will happen if they stay."

"Are you not scared, Mam?"

She turned to him. "I am. Particularly of MacGillouvry – but I'm more frightened of what would happen if we leave."

*

Catrìona's mind was filled with fear. Each day seemed precious. The morning light behind Sìdh Chaillean, the cry of the buzzard, the smell of the gorse, the clack of the loom as she worked.

She found herself in the Black Wood. She couldn't remember how she got there, hadn't intended to go. She wandered through the trees. Stopping to lean against one, her legs so tired, her body crumpled against the warm trunk and she sank down between two large roots, leaning her head against the rough bark. A howl came from her belly. Birds flew away in alarm. Tears were falling. How could she leave here? Her life was tied to this place, there was nowhere else she wanted to be. The tree held steady behind, shielding, supporting her. *Defend yourself*, were the words she heard.

Her arm was resting on a piece of smooth wood. At first she thought it was another root but it came loose when she touched it. It was about a foot long and straight. When she picked it up it felt comfortable in her right hand. She pulled herself up from the ground, still holding the piece of wood. She was prepared.

*

It was still light and she should have been working or baking but she wanted to do neither. She sat outside the house, gazing across the loch to Beinn Labhair. It was a beautiful evening, warm light lingering on the mountain tops. She couldn't live without the mountains around her.

Daibhidh was walking up the track. He came to sit beside her on the bench.

"We've been through some hard times, Catrìona, but nothing as terrible as this."

"I dream of the constables coming in the middle of the night. I sleep with a stick by my side. I can no longer sing. It's as if my soul has dried up."

"We must hope for a miracle. Perhaps the priest will intervene when he sees families leaving?"

"He will not." She shook her head, unable to say more.

He put his hand on her shoulder. "I remember when Fionn had the accident. I was due to marry Annie and I turned her down. I couldn't abandon my brother. You talked to her and tried to explain. Then she wasn't so unhappy. I haven't forgotten it, or all the other ways you have been my friend. I can stay here at night. I will sleep on heather. If something happens you won't be alone."

She turned to him, realising what he was offering – protection, maybe something more –wanting desperately to say yes, just for the comfort of it, but it wouldn't change the fact that they were both going to be homeless soon.

"Thank you Daibhidh, but I'm strong enough."

The pain in her back grew worse, making it hard to sleep. Piling more heather on the bed made no difference. She'd grown thinner, bones showing pale near the surface of her skin. In the morning it was hard to rouse herself but Brèagha still had to be milked. If things were as usual she would be making ready, salting the vegetables and potatoes, making cheese, storing food in case of a bad winter. The last had been cold but crisp, sunsets and frost, not much rain and few real gales, until the one that had killed the old laird.

A week passed, and the date on the writ grew closer.

Catrìona talked to Màiri every day, wanting to clutch onto her friend for fear they'd be separated.

Màiri said, "I've no relatives near here. My sister says

I can stay with her in Glasgow but I would rather lose my right foot. The stories I've heard about the noise and dirt. I'll go when they kick me out but not before."

The MacDougalls were leaving. They had already sold the cow and the chickens and now they were piling a cart with whatever would fit on, tools, furniture, though the largest items had to be left behind. Catrìona walked down to the house as they were putting the last stools on top, the legs splayed out like some upturned beast. Dougall MacDougall lifted his youngest daughter onto the cart; the others would walk.

Catrìona had watched them grow. "Where will you go?"

"To Perth. I have some family there who can take us in, though not for long as they're already overwhelmed."

"I'm sorry to say goodbye." She held back tears, not wanting the children to see her cry – they were already distressed enough.

"I hope that you can stay here," he said. "God bless you all."

She waved as they set off down the track, the children following the cart as it bumped over the stones.

*

Catrìona had no sense of a life after Torr Uaine. No house or place came to her mind, only darkness – a kind of void. She was in pain, in her body and across her chest where her heart was.

There was only one last thing to try. She didn't want to for she hated him, but she must persuade MacGillouvry to let them stay. She would beg, for the alternative was unthinkable. Whatever happened she had to make sure

Eòin and Seònaid and the baby were going to be looked after. It would be terrible for Seònaid to be uprooted so close to giving birth.

MacGillouvry lived near Kinloch. He owned a large farm and had many men working for him. He had a wife, but it was said they had no children.

On a cold, bright day Catrìona put on her best dress and began the walk to Kinloch. She hadn't told Eòin, who would tell her not to go. The birch leaves had fallen, scattering yellow and brown over the banks and the water. Any other day she would have stopped to admire the colours but she was sick with fear and uncertainty at what she would achieve. When she'd visited the laird she'd had confidence in the knowledge of her secret. Now she had almost nothing, only the barest thread of hope and her desperation.

She asked at the inn for directions and the landlord told her to cross the river and take the first turning up a track on the left. He looked at her curiously as if he wanted to ask about her business with the factor but said nothing.

The house was large, and solidly built. To the side was a stable. The black head of a horse looked out from a stall. A man led a cow into a large barn to the side of the stable, but he didn't notice her.

She lifted the knocker and after a second's hesitation let it fall.

A woman came to the door; Catrìona assumed she was Mrs MacGillouvry. She was wearing a Paisley patterned dress with a dark blue and cream shawl. "Can I help you?"

An English accent.

"Good morning. Is your husband, Mr MacGillouvry, at home?"

The woman smiled and said, "You've mistaken me, I'm afraid, I'm not Mrs MacGillouvry, I'm her sister, visiting here for the first time. They've gone for a drive in the trap this morning but will be back soon, I think. Would you like to wait? My name is Emily Taylor." The woman was friendly, as if pleased to have company.

"I am Catrìona MacGregor. I don't want to disturb you."

"It's no trouble. I'm still recovering from my journey. I took the train to Perth station but the many miles by carriage were very rough. Take a seat. If they're not back soon I can give them a message. You didn't say why you were visiting?"

"I have a query."

The woman nodded and sat in a chair opposite. Catrìona wanted desperately to be gone. To cover her awkwardness she said, "I admire your shawl, it's beautifully made."

"Thank you, I bought it in Edinburgh where I stopped for the night. It is light but very warm."

Catriona nodded. "I'm a weaver myself, I don't have such fine wool but I make similar shawls. I made this one." She was wearing one of dark green with thin stripes of red and yellow – not a MacGregor tartan, for that would rile MacGillouvry.

"It's pretty. Perhaps if I stay long enough you would make one similar for me?"

At that moment there was the sound of hooves and wheels on cobbles.

"Ah, that's lucky, they're back."

Emily got up and went to the door, saying. "I've been entertaining one of your visitors, John."

Catrìona stood, clutching her bonnet, wondering what would happen when he saw her. He came through the door, followed by his wife. He stopped when he saw Catrìona. "You."

The sister looked from one to the other. "Is there a problem?"

He glared at her. "This is not your business, Emily." Turning again to Catriona. "Please go, I've nothing to say to you."

"But John, Mrs MacGregor has a question for you," Emily said.

"She's a troublemaker – her son assaulted me."

Mrs MacGillouvry was looking at Catrìona with dislike.

"Please. I must speak to you," Catrìona said.

He pointed to the door. "Outside. You can have a minute of my time."

Emily looked confused. Catrìona walked out of the door with her head bowed.

Standing in the yard before him, she said, "Please, sir. It's coming into winter, we can't leave Torr Uaine now, some of us have nowhere to go. Please give us until next spring at least."

"You deserve no favours from me."

"I'm begging you – let us stay until next year."

He looked at her with disdain. "And what can you offer in return?"

During the walk there Catrìona had been thinking. She shook at the thought of what she must offer. "I can sell the cow. She is worth twenty pounds."

"And what about the other tenants, will that pay their rents too?"

"It will help."

"The process is already in motion. The laird needs the land for his new venture. The builders have already been commissioned for the lodge. To agree would mean a delay."

He paused, looking at her so intently that she stepped backwards. "There may be a way. I believe you have a loom?"

She looked at him, fearful of what he was going to say next.

"My wife has a desire to learn to weave. If you make her a gift of it I will approach the laird to ask if the tenants may have more time."

A sharp pain jabbed at her side, making it hard to stay upright. Her joy, her livelihood, her wedding present from Donnchadh.

"Is there nothing else that I can offer? That's the way I earn my living."

He shook his head, "No. That's the answer."

For a few moments she battled with herself, wanting desperately to say no but knowing that, if it meant they could stay until the baby was born, she must say yes.

"Then I agree." She felt sick inside. "Will you cancel the writs for the first of December?"

"There's no need for that. You have my word. I'll ask the laird to give you until the first of March."

On the way home Catrìona leant against the wall at the head of the loch. A thick mist hung over the water. A farmer passing asked if she needed any help but she said she was just taking a rest. As she struggled home she decided she must also sell Brèagha, to raise money for Eòin in case he needed it. There would be no more fresh milk but she could manage with water from the burn.

20

Brèagha shifted and mooed quietly as Catriona leant against the side of her warm flank pulling on the udders. She'd bought her soon after Donnchadh had died. Their last cow was old and Catrìona had let Eòin choose another; the farmer said that she was small and might not produce much milk but Eòin loved her from the start so they took her home. He'd named her Brèagha. She'd given Catrìona a few bruises at first but after a while they made a connection.

Sometimes, after Donnchadh died, Catrìona would go into the byre, away from where Eòin slept, sit with Brèagha and cry. Brèagha would look at her with dark brown eyes and then turn back to her feed.

With a heavy heart Catrìona went to see Eòin. "Can we talk alone?" she said.

Seònaid was rearranging the bed and did not hear her. Once outside he asked, "Is something wrong?"

"Will you take Brèagha to the market for me?"

"Is she not producing?"

"She still yields but I need money. I've been to see MacGillouvry."

"What business have you with him?"

"We made an agreement. If I give him the loom he will give us more time."

Eòin stared at her. "What have you done, Mam?"

"Seònaid may give birth as the writ comes into effect. She's already vulnerable. If I do this, MacGillouvry will give us until the first of March. It's worth that, surely."

"And you believe him?"

"He gave me his word."

Eòin laughed. "His word means nothing. He's an evil man."

"He's cruel but perhaps not dishonest."

"You can't be sure of that!"

It was rare that they disagreed. His face showed his anger and disappointment.

"It's better to leave than to do a deal with that man. I think Seònaid should hear about this."

Seònaid was sitting on a stool stirring the soup. Her stomach bulged under her dark blue skirt.

"Mam has been negotiating a deal with MacGillouvry."

Seònaid looked from one to the other. "What do you mean?"

"The writ says we must leave by the first of December. I've bought us some more time – we now have until March," said Catrìona.

"That's good, isn't it?" Seònaid said.

Eòin put his hand on her shoulder. "We can't negotiate with that man. I'm sorry."

Seònaid stood up. "But where will we go? I cannot go back to my father's house, even if he would have us – I'd be scared for the baby."

"We won't go there. Besides, the laird's curse might soon affect the rest of the strath. We must stay here and fight. I believe we can defeat MacGillouvry. He acts as if he is in charge but so far he has done nothing."

"You'd risk our baby?"

"Don't you see, Eòin?" interrupted Catrìona. "That's why I wanted the time, so Seònaid will be safe."

"I don't know what to think," Seònaid said and began to cry.

Eòin put his arm around her. "This is our home – they cannot take it."

"I did what I thought was best. I'm sorry if you think I was wrong. I'll go now," Catrìona said.

She stood outside the cottage, wrestling with herself, wondering if Eòin was right and MacGillouvry had lied to her. Needing advice, she went to find Màiri.

"What have you done, Catrìona? Confronting the laird was one thing, but make a deal with MacGillouvry? You cannot think he'll keep his word."

"I need to believe it. The thought of leaving Torr Uaine is terrible. I'll lose Eòin and Seònaid and I'll lose you." She couldn't look Màiri in the eye. "I can't bear that." Grief came over her. Màiri pulled up a stool and sat next to her, leaning her head close to Catrìona's.

"Nor I, but we have our pride and we can fight. Who's to say that the constables will do the laird's bidding? Some of them are our neighbour's sons. Do not give your loom away. Please."

Deep down she knew Màiri was right.

"I don't want to. It's all that I have left of Donnchadh."

Màiri nodded. "Then you must not. Now listen. I want to tell you a story. Something I should have told you a long time ago."

"I'd like that."

"He built my house."

"Who did?"

"Aonghas, my husband."

175

Catrìona hadn't heard his name in a long time. Màiri had spoken of him once or twice when they first met but never again.

"I didn't know that."

"He was a good builder. It's solid, weatherproof, small but just right. He said he wanted me to be safe. Chose one of the best spots in the village, high but sheltered from the wind, near the burn for water."

She paused and Catrìona asked what she'd never asked before. "What really happened to him, Mhàiri?"

"He disappeared one night, as I told you. He went out walking and didn't return. Never told me where he was going. I was distraught for a while, looked everywhere, I was always asking people if they'd seen him. I thought he'd drowned or got lost on the moor. Then years later I heard word from someone in Pitlochry. He'd seen Aonghas with a woman and two small bairns."

"Why did you never tell me?"

Màiri looked down at her worn hands. "I was ashamed. I couldn't have children; that's why he went. For four years after we were married nothing happened, not even a miscarriage, and he accused me of not being a proper woman. I've helped others but no one could help me."

"I am so sorry, Mhàiri. It must have been hard when you found out the truth."

"I was angry and hurt. When I think about him my anger is still there."

"Did you never want to marry again?"

"We're still married – he committed bigamy. I wouldn't do that. And what would be the purpose if I couldn't have children?"

"I'm sorry to hear the truth. I preferred the stories that

people made up about him. Thank you for helping me and others so much."

Màiri sighed and said, "I wish I could have done more for your daughters."

"You did what you could, no one could have saved them."

*

Catrìona wrote to MacGillouvry and said that she was sorry for any inconvenience but she'd decided to keep the loom. Her hand was shaking as she gave the letter to the postmaster.

She milked Brèagha for the last time. She didn't want to alarm her so she sang, a quiet song with a pretty tune. Brèagha had helped to keep her and Eòin alive. Catrìona liked the warmth and the sound of rustling at night as the cow turned around in the byre.

When she'd finished she stroked the soft flank. "Thank you for all you've given me. If there was any other way, I would keep you with me, but there's trouble coming."

Brèagha puffed through her nostrils and went on eating.

Daibhidh came by. He'd offered to take Brèagha to the market to save Catrìona the upset. "I'm sorry you have to be parted from her. She's always been good." He took the rope from her hand. "Are you ready, Catrìona?"

She nodded, unable to speak.

He began the walk down the track. Brèagha turned her head back once as if she knew it was time. Catrìona watched, shading her eyes from the sun, as the two of them disappeared over the hill. Then she went back inside and cried – for Brèagha, for herself, and for all in Torr Uaine.

She awoke in the night and listened to the silence penetrating the wall. No other living thing under her roof, Eòin gone, Brèagha gone. She got up and went outside. There was a crescent moon and thousands of stars scattered across the sky, on and on and on to the dark horizon.

21

ROSE

Rose was waiting for an email from Bridget. Desperation pulled at her like the hand of an insistent child, needing to know what had happened to Catrìona.

To occupy her mind, she pinned all the drawings and watercolours from her sketchbooks to the wall, turning the cottage into a temporary studio. The vivid green moss on fallen stones, the twisted shapes of the Caledonian pines, the reflection of the hills in the loch. A drawing of the eagle by the rowan tree with one wing spread out, sketches of rocks, lochans and heather. She picked up the shuttle and laid it against her cheek. She could feel Catrìona's hands, warm and rough from planting, weaving, washing.

She was recreating Catrìona's life, one tiny piece at a time. Making art helped her to make sense of things. It was a way to find a purpose and point to all the hard and irrational things that happened in life but for this it seemed ineffective, as if she was merely scratching the surface of what was a huge and widespread injustice.

Later she sat by the fire reading. There was a knock on the door, which made her jump. She hesitated, not wanting to answer because it was getting late, then she heard Tòmas's voice.

"Rose? Are you there?"

She went to the door.

"I tried calling earlier."

"I've been working, my phone was off. Come in." She was aware that her hair was tangled and wild.

They went into the living room, where he saw the drawings and stopped. "These are beautiful!"

"Thanks, they're just sketches really."

"I love this one of the eagle."

"It's such a sad image."

He looked at her. "Are you OK?"

"Not really. I found something disturbing in the diaries."

"Do you want to talk about it?"

She shook her head. "I'm still trying to come to terms with it. I'll tell you sometime – it's made me feel as if I'm on shaky ground, even more than I usually do."

"I understand. I often feel like that. Weirdly it's only on water that I feel completely grounded."

She was glad he was there, realising that she'd spent too much time alone. "Do you want to stay for a drink? I've got some whisky."

"Aye, OK."

She poured him a glass. They chatted about art and music and which artists inspired them. She told him about her favourite artists, sculptors mainly and almost all, but not exclusively, women – Rebecca Horn, Cornelia Parker, Eva Hesse. He told her about musicians he liked, Julie Fowlis, King Creosote.

After a while he said, "It's getting late, I'd better get back."

"Don't go," she said, surprising herself. "Stay here."

"Is that what you want?"

"Yes."

The ceiling in the bedroom sloped steeply. There wasn't enough room for two people to stand up so they undressed and lay on the bed naked, close together, looking at each other. Whatever they were about to do, it wasn't a fling. Their bodies were similar in length – her skin was paler. She put her hand on his chest, tentative. He put his arms around her and his fingers caught in the tangle of her hair. She kissed him, noticing the shape of his forehead and the colour of his eyes and the sound of the rain falling on the skylight. He was intense and serious, as if putting his whole mind and body into being with her. She responded with equal intensity, a voice in her head saying *It's OK, you can trust this man.*

Afterwards they lay side by side, holding hands.

"I wasn't expecting that," she said.

"Nor me. I'm glad you came to find your ancestors."

She turned to him. "I am too, though I wasn't looking for anybody, for this."

"Me neither but maybe that's the best way."

In the morning when they woke they curled up together. She turned to him. "I haven't had a relationship for a while. The last one ended badly. It's quite hard for me to trust people." She wanted him to know the truth about her. "I think it's because of what happened to my dad."

He propped himself up on one arm to look at her. "What about your dad?"

"He disappeared."

"Oh. When was that?"

"I was ten. He went out on a boat and didn't come back."

"That's awful."

"They never found his body so we didn't even have a funeral. Only a memorial, a year later, when they said there was no chance of finding him alive. Even when you get told that you can't really believe it."

"That sounds really hard."

"What made it worse was that we didn't talk about it. Mum must have been sad but she never showed it. She was angry quite often – I think she felt abandoned. I had to go to secondary school that year and I always felt weird, different. It was hard for my brother, Cal, too."

"I can't imagine what that's like. Both my parents are still alive. They're not together but at least I know where they are."

"Maybe that's why I'm looking for my history – trying to find some answers. I should let him go. I know I should."

She turned away suddenly. Putting her face in the pillow she sobbed, a deep sound that scared her. He pulled her close. "It's OK, Rose. I'm here."

She rarely talked about her dad, had grown used to suppressing any feelings about his disappearance and thought she'd forgotten how to cry. Soon she stopped but in those few minutes it seemed something had changed. She felt lighter, as if there might be some kind of future.

They got up and she made them breakfast, then he said, "I better get to work. You know Rose, I meant it when I said I wanted you to stay here."

"It seems impossible. I have a job in London, I'm definitely not wanted here by the Menzies, I'm causing them trouble."

"Good, that's what's needed. You're a fighter, a Scot at heart."

"Do you think so?"

"Aye. Can I see you later?"

"OK."

After he'd gone, she opened the back door so the wind blew in from the hills. Her body felt alive and full of joy. She tidied up and hummed to herself, thinking about what he'd said. It seemed unlikely, though not impossible.

There was a knock on the door. She opened it and saw Fergusson. She went to shut it but he said, "You need to hear what I've got to say."

He didn't have his gun and was standing a few feet away from the door.

"See this?" He waved a piece of paper at her.

"What is it?"

"It's addressed to Aileen and Ruaraidh MacDonald. She's your friend, isn't she? That's a nice wee cottage they have with their daughter. They've done it up well. It would be a shame if they got evicted. That's what this is. Notice. If you don't back off it will be in the post."

She felt cold. It was exactly what Aileen had been frightened of. She couldn't see what was on the letter but had no doubt that he meant it.

"You English, you think you're clever. Most people here like the sporting estates. They bring in money. You need to give up your crusade and get back home."

She was holding tight onto the door. "Can you go now please?"

"Your choice. You've got until tomorrow to get out. And don't tell your boyfriend about this – it will only make it worse."

Rose went back into the cottage and shut the door, leaning on it, her legs shaky. It would be terrible if Aileen got evicted; she had a child and a wonderful life there. She didn't know what to do. She looked around the cottage. It had started to feel a bit like her home – she loved being there, surrounded by nature, hearing the wind and the birds in the trees, the amazing changing light on the hills. Some new friends nearby.

She sat in the living room, staring into space, trying to decide what to do. She couldn't call Tòmas. Maybe Fergusson was bluffing. She hadn't seen what was in the letter, but she didn't think she could ignore his threat.

There was no choice. She went upstairs and began to pack her things. She brought the case down and started to take the drawings off the walls. It was still early; if she went soon, she'd have time to drive to Perth, drop the car off and catch the train to Edinburgh, then London. She took down the last drawing and the room was bare again. It seemed brutal. One minute she was singing, the next she was leaving. No time to say goodbye to anyone. Seumas, Aileen, Lily, Angus, Tòmas.

She began writing a note to Tòmas.

"Really sorry to leave without saying goodbye. I can't stay. Some people don't want me here. I really liked…." What to say? In the end she put "getting to know you." That was the truth. She didn't know what else to write so she left it like that. She couldn't tell him why she was going as he might confront Fergusson and then Aileen could be under threat.

She packed the car and then went down to the loch. It was breezy and the surface of the water was covered with small waves. The family of ducks was bobbing over them. She sat on a tree stump and hugged her knees, soaking in the mountains and hills, the sound of the breeze in the trees. She tried to imagine being back in London but couldn't.

The sound of a car nearby disturbed her thoughts. The engine cut out and a voice called out. "*Mhadainn Mhath*."

She stood up. It was Seumas. "Are you enjoying the view?"

"It's lovely – so peaceful."

"Aye, it is. You've picked a fine place to live."

She was about to say she wouldn't be staying but he said, "Well I must getting on, I'll be seeing you and Aileen any day I expect."

On the way through Kinloch she stopped at Tòmas's house and posted the note through the letterbox. As an afterthought she dropped the keys to the cottage through too. The journey home was long and depressing. She turned off her phone.

The next day she picked up Tòmas's messages. When she called him, their conversation was stilted. She told him she couldn't explain why and said sorry several times. In the end he'd said, "It's OK, Rose. I don't want you to do something you don't want to."

22

CATRÌONA

It was Sunday. Five days before the date on the writ. There'd been no visit from the priest to offer his people any solace. Catrìona didn't want to attend kirk but she wanted to meet with the folk from Ardlarich and the other villages. She walked with Daibhidh, Mairead and the baby and Jessie.

Mairead said, "Alasdair refused to come – he says he no longer has any belief in God."

"MacGillouvry has withdrawn his offer for my land. The man who wanted to buy it grew tired of waiting. I lost my chance." Daibhidh shrugged. "I had some regret for a moment but I couldn't have done a deal with the devil."

Mairead shifted the baby higher in the shawl. "We've looked after this land – it's fertile due to our efforts. What more do they want from us?"

"They want us gone. We're nothing to them, mere grains of barley that can be brushed away and forgotten," Catrìona said. "We must show them we're more than that."

"You're still hopeful that we can win?" Mairead asked.

Catrìona paused for a moment. "I think so. We're determined. Others will help too – it could be their villages next year."

Jessie was silent, not skipping or talking. Then she

said, "There's no other place on earth as beautiful as this."

Her mother laughed. "You've been nowhere else, Jessie."

"I've been to other places and I believe she may be right," Daibhidh said.

The priest didn't raise a smile as the villagers filed into the kirk. The sermon was unrelated to their concerns. Instead of listening to his words Catrìona looked around her, at the whitewashed walls, the smooth flagstones and the altar at which she'd been married by a different priest; a kinder man, a long time ago.

The priest paused after finishing the sermon, his head bowed. When he lifted it there was a look of sorrow on his face.

"You've all sinned. By refusing to pay your rents you're bringing trouble and sorrow to the strath. I cannot condone your behaviour. The laird wants only what's best for his land. Now we shall have prayers and I hope that you'll rethink your actions."

Catrìona found his coldness hard to believe. Anger and sadness flooded through her. She didn't belong there, it was no longer nourishment for her soul. She put her hand on Mairead's arm and said quietly, "I'm leaving – come with me." Rising from the pew she began walking down the aisle. She heard Mairead get up, the baby whimpering. She passed others and nodded at them. They looked at her and realising what she was doing, began to rise too.

The priest's voice followed them. "You're foolish. Leaving here will not help."

Catrìona lifted the latch on the door and went out. The people followed her. They were still silent. She stood under the spreading oak outside the churchyard, Daibhidh next to her. The others gathered around.

She looked around at the familiar faces, young and old. "We're on our own, that's clear. We only have a few days left. Some have already gone. They're worried for their bairns and have places to go. Those of us who can't leave must stick together. If we stand firm there's a chance they'll change their minds or at least give us until Spring to make other arrangements. The sheriff is not a bad man. We don't own this land but we've looked after and nourished it. We deserve to be treated with respect."

People were nodding. A man from Ardlarich spoke. "We're with you. If they remove you from Torr Uaine it'll be a crime and if one is committed against you it's against all of us."

"The notice is for Friday the first of December. If you can be spared from your work then we need you here. We don't want trouble, only to stop them from taking our homes."

All around agreed. "Aye Catrìona." "We'll be there. As the sun rises."

*

Catrìona had finished another shawl and taken it to Kinloch to be sold, collecting the money that the shop owed her. With the money she received from the sale of Brèagha she had twenty-five pounds. She made enquiries about the cost of a passage to Canada and was told it would be six pounds for a ticket for two people.

The loom looked naked without any fabric. She ran her hands over the smooth wood, remembering when Donnchadh had brought it home on the pony and trap. She'd taught herself to use it. Now it was as if the shuttle were part of her body, attached to her hands. She could weave a shawl in half the time of most. She wanted Jessie to have the loom when she herself died. That might not be possible as the Frasers had no spare room in their house. Still, Jessie was growing and in a few years' time she might have a husband and house of her own.

Waiting for the day was hard. Catrìona swept the floor and hung all the pans, shook out the blankets and polished the table, wanting to be ready for whatever was going to happen. In the moments when she sat for a rest, she could not help but cry, thinking about her long life there, with Donnchadh and without, the laughter, music, the work and the sorrow.

On the night of 30th November she went to Eòin's house. Seònaid had gone to stay with the MacDonalds in Ardlarich. She hadn't wanted to go but Eòin persuaded her, saying that she should not have to witness any trouble.

"Are you prepared, Mam?"

She sat on a stool. The fire was lit and a pan of soup was simmering. "I'm as ready as I can be. We'll try to negotiate, at least they must give us longer. When they see how many of us are still here. Whatever happens, you must avoid MacGillouvry. He's a dangerous man and he wishes you ill."

"I'll do my best."

They ate soup together. She could almost believe it was an ordinary day, before Eòin was married. The wind was getting up, blowing around the corner of the croft but the house was snug, the wooden beams solid. Seònaid had made it look nice. There was a coloured rug by the bed and the pretty wooden horse that Eòin had carved for her was on the window sill.

"You've grown into a fine man, Eòin. It was hard, losing your father so early, but you've made much of your life."

"That's because of you, Mam. You worked hard to show me the way. I know I was difficult after father died. It was hard to express what I felt.'

"I know, son. For a few years we were both lost but now we're found. Only now we're to lose again." She stared into the smoky fire, lost in thought.

He touched her on the arm. "Go home and rest, for we must be up early tomorrow."

The tenants gathered at Catrìona's house at first light. Eòin and Màiri arrived first, then Jessie with her father and two brothers. Mairead had stayed at home with the baby. They were silent as they walked down to the entrance to the village. One or two gathered stones. Catrìona held her stick by her side.

As they reached the gap in the wall Catrìona saw a large group of tenants coming up the track. They'd come from Ardlarich and Annat as well as the south side. Soon they were all together, maybe one hundred or more. When she saw how many were there, she stood straighter. There was no time to discuss how to organise because over the noise of people talking came the sound of horses' hooves thudding up the track.

Catrìona stood in the centre of the crowd. Her heart was pounding fast. There was a low gasp as they saw how many were there. Four horses. Astride them were the sheriff, the fiscal, MacGillouvry and the priest. She'd not seen him on a horse before. Behind them were at least twenty constables on foot.

The sheriff rode towards them and reined in his horse.

"Good morning to you. I see that there are more people here than live in Torr Uaine. I hope you're not here to cause trouble." There was murmuring among the tenants. "As you are aware, today is the date of the writ. You've had a month to find other places to live. The laird needs his land."

Catrìona stepped forward. "We cannot leave."

"But madam, what do you mean? You're clearly not incapable. You have two arms and two legs. You can pick up your possessions and take them away."

MacGillouvry pushed his horse towards her. "This woman leads the troublemakers – a MacGregor." He spat the words out. "Clear the way for the constables."

The sheriff intervened. "Mrs MacGregor. You've been treated with respect. You were asked to pay an increase in rent, which you refused to do. You were given time to reconsider, then, when you didn't do that, you were given a month's notice to remove yourselves, which although a few of your number have done, the majority have not. You must realise that the law is on our side."

"Sir, we cannot afford lawyers. We have the law of the land instead. An ancient one that's been passed down through generations. It's unwritten but strong and it decrees that you have no right to make us go. Who's to say who owns the land? Only God knows that, surely."

The crowd cheered at her words.

The priest said, "That's heathen talk – you know nothing of the mind of God. These people are becoming more and more unruly; last Sunday, for instance, they walked out of the kirk before the service was ended."

There was jeering. "Call yourself a priest." "You should be ashamed." "Would you leave your own house?"

The sheriff raised his hand. "You must clear the way now or the law will do whatever is necessary to gain access to the village."

Daibhidh said, "My house is the first on the track, my brother is sick in there."

"The constables have been told to start at the top and work down, now make way."

Catrìona turned to the priest. "I beg you to stop this."

"No, madam, that I cannot do."

The villagers stood firm – a ring around the village. Catrìona took Eòin's hand. She began to sing.

An srath dham buan mi
Tha mo spiorad fhathast ann
Bho chreag gu monadh
Bho allt gu coille
Chan fhalbh mi gu dèo

Eòin sang with her. She heard Daibhidh's deep voice join in, then that of Jessie. More voices joined, swelling over the strath, as the men on the horses sat looking grim faced.

When they finished there was a silence as if Torr Uaine held its breath. Catrìona's fist was clenched around the stick.

The sheriff said, "Enough." He turned to the constables, who were standing with their batons held at the ready. "Do your job."

The men moved forward, pushing Catrìona and the others aside. A baton pressed into her, hurting her breasts, and she stumbled out of the way.

The constables started up the hill with MacGillouvry at their head. He called to them, "The MacGregors' houses first."

Eòin began to run and the villagers surged after, trying to get ahead. Catrìona went as fast as she could. When she got to the top of the hill Eòin and others were in front of her house, blocking the door. Across the burn others were doing the same at Màiri's house.

Catrìona stood with Eòin. MacGillouvry drove his horse forwards. A huge black head and chest came at her, astride the horse, MacGillouvry's face was full of rage. She jumped out of the way but he raised a stick and hit her on the shoulder. She cried out and then heard a shout, recognising the voice as Eòin's, saw him jump up and pull MacGillouvry from the horse.

They began to fight. Catrìona jumped forward to try to stop them but a constable came at her, grabbed her hair and kicked her. She felt a sharp pain as something hit her on the side of the head. She fell forwards, face in the muddy ground.

She pulled herself up, dizzy and wanting to vomit, her sight blurred. Two constables were taking furniture from her house and throwing it to the ground. She staggered towards the door. The fire had been put out and the embers kicked around. One of them raised his truncheon. She screamed out "No!" as he brought it down on the loom. The wood groaned. As he raised his truncheon again she threw herself in front of the precious frame but he thrust her out of the way. The warp threads were holding the pieces of the loom together. The constable attacked it with a sort of madness until it collapsed on the floor in a twisted, broken heap.

The other man had a stick wrapped with straw and heather and set it alight – he was holding it up inside the roof and Catrìona watched in horror as the flames spread quickly, filling the room with smoke. The constables left. Catrìona tried to beat out the flames with a rug but it was hopeless. She turned, desperate to get her purse which was in her father's bowl in a far corner. The air was thick with smoke so she put her shawl over her mouth and with her arms outstretched she went forward, stumbling over a stool until finally her hand grasped it. She staggered outside, coughing and choking.

All around furniture was strewn across the grass. Clusters of people were trying to save what they could. Columns of smoke were coming from the roofs of houses. The throbbing in her head continued. She climbed the hill and found Màiri lying outside her house. Her dress and shawl were torn and there was blood in her grey hair.

Catrìona bent beside her. "Mhàiri, what have they done?"

Màiri opened her eyes and said, "My house. Where's Aonghas?"

Catrìona helped her up and moved her away from the house. "I'll be back as soon as I can with some water."

Eòin came running up the track. "Thank God you're alive. I swear they're trying to kill people." He had a cut across his nose and his hand was bloody. "The constables are after me for attacking MacGillouvry."

"They'll sentence you to a long imprisonment, maybe even transportation. Leave now. Find Seònaid and go."

"But where can we go? We have no money and Seònaid can't travel far."

"I have money. You must go to your uncle in Canada. Robert MacDonald will take you to Glasgow. There's a ship sailing in two days for Quebec."

194

"You must come too."

"I'm too old to travel and Màiri needs me. My place is here."

"My place is here too, Mam."

She stroked his cheek. "This is a cruel time, son. You and Seònaid must do what you need to survive. I've money from selling Brèagha." She put the purse in his hands. "It's enough for your passage and for you and Seònaid to start a new life in Canada."

She put her arms around him, the person she'd made and loved for so many precious years – not wanting to let him go. He was shaking and she heard his sobs. "My love will always be with you. Go over the top to Ardlarich, straight to MacDonald's house, do not stop to say goodbye to anyone. I'll tell the constables you're heading for Kinloch."

"I can't leave you here."

"I'll take care of myself and Màiri. Don't worry. Now go, please."

"Goodbye then, Mam."

"Goodbye, son."

The expression on his face tore at her heart.

He kissed her on the cheek and then let her go. He disappeared behind the house then after a minute he reappeared, running along the high path towards Ardlarich.

She leant against the wall of her field, shocked by the sudden separation, wondering if she'd ever feel whole again. The constables moved from house to house, pulling people and furniture out, setting fire to the thatch. She buried her father's bowl under the turf near the door to her blackened house, hoping that one day she might come back. Then, stumbling over the heather, she found Màiri lying by the burn, clutching a broken bottle of medicine. Catrìona knelt beside her and held her hand. The sound of the water tumbling over the stones drowned out the noise in the village.

23

ROSE

'Bell and Hathaway.' The sign on what used to be Jim's Café was silver on dark grey. The door was open and Rose could see that the back had been extended. There were elegant grey and orange chairs and long mirrors along the wall. The photograph of the Blue Mosque had gone.

London was loud, brash – she disappeared back into it, her anonymity familiar. The college was busy, a new intake of students wanting support with their first projects. At last, the final part of Catrìona's diary arrived. It was short and didn't tell her much.

> *November. Brèagha has been sold to raise money.*
> *Thick snow falls on Torr Uaine. The nights are cold.*
> *We have tried to persuade them to let us stay but I am*
> *fearful that they will not.*
> *We are waiting. We are scared.*

There were no further entries. The notes about daily life and dye recipes had been abandoned. The eviction must have happened soon after. She'd read about the violence. The women had often been on the front line, trying to defend their homes. She imagined the police, or the army, riding the rough loch road before it was tarmacked, the villagers trying to defend their houses. The shouting and the children's cries, the thud of wood on flesh.

Eòin and Seònaid must have gone to Canada after this. On the family tree their child was called Donald. Jack was Donald's grandson. Somehow the diary had ended up in Jack's possession. Perhaps a relative or friend had sent it to Canada after Catrìona died. She wondered if Donald had been born in Scotland or Canada, or on the boat in between. She thought of the newborn, held tight by Seònaid, his first moments of life spent in the dark hold of a creaking ship in a storm.

Jack had come to England in 1940 with the Canadian army. That much she knew. The Canadians were stationed on the south coast for two years, bored and desperate for action, but they couldn't have envisaged the terrible slaughter of the Dieppe Raid.

After her dad disappeared Jack had visited them and Rose's relationship with him began at this time. He'd told Mum that it was his fault Dad had gone. The war had made a mess of him. Most of his friends had been killed on a single day on the French beaches. He'd survived, injured, and afterwards had nightmares and sometimes fits of rage. He said when Dad was born it got worse. He couldn't stand looking at this baby boy, thinking of all the young men who'd died. He'd walked out, frightened of doing something terrible, she supposed that now they'd call it PTSD. Later he married Susan but didn't have any more children.

These violent events had repercussions that were still being felt generations later. By Dad, Cal and herself.

Cal's leg was out of plaster. The flat looked clean though shabby. He was working as a volunteer at an arts project for children, teaching music.

"I like it. The children call me Mr Cal. I say it's Cal but Mr has stuck. There might be a paid job in a couple of months."

That's good."

"What happened in Scotland?"

She showed him photos of Torr Uaine and the portrait at Creag Dhubh.

"Who's that?"

"Anthony Menzies, ancestor of Robert Menzies, the current landowner. Do you see the likeness?"

"What are you saying?"

She told him about Seònaid – the rape and the baby.

"You see, we're descended from the same family that cleared the community in Torr Uaine."

"God, that's weird. Did Granddad know?"

"I think so, though he said he didn't remember much Gaelic. There was no one in England who spoke it. Perhaps that's why he wanted me to have the diaries. Dad can't have known. He'd have said, sometime when he was drunk – 'We're all children of the bastard', or something like that."

"Did you confront Robert Menzies?"

"He refused to acknowledge it."

"Denial is their only defence. No wonder we're fucked up." Cal threw an apple core towards the waste bin but it missed its target.

"It's hard to get my head round what it all means," she said. "Most of the real history must be hidden. People were probably too busy trying to survive to record what happened. It's really lucky we were given the diary but I still want to find out what happened to Catrìona."

*

Rose missed the loch and the mountains, the wind at night and the cry of the buzzard. She missed Tòmas. She sent him a card with one of her drawings but stopped herself from apologising. He texted to thank her but there was no other communication.

In the studio a train passed by on the track. She shivered. Although it was only October it was already cold. Lee had left the studio and moved to Kent a few weeks earlier, no longer able to afford her rented flat in London. Rose needed to find someone else for the space but wasn't keen on sharing with someone she didn't know. The studio had lost the sense of being her home. She was starting a new piece of work, a clay relief based on her drawings of Torr Uaine.

There was a quiet knock on the door. Putting down the lump of clay she went to open it. Tòmas stood there, a backpack on one shoulder and an awkward smile on his face. "Hello Rose."

It took her a moment to speak. "How did you find me?"

"Sorry if I gave you a shock. You told me once what the studio block was called and I tracked it down. I wanted to see you." He was hesitating in the doorway.

"Come in. I've got clay all over me, hang on." She went to the sink and quickly rinsed her hands. Turning she crossed the studio and hugged him.

"I've missed you," she said.

"Have you?"

"Yes."

She made them coffee and they sat on the two old wooden chairs.

"Why did you leave like that?"

She looked down, worried about what would happen if she told him. Then she made a decision. "I wanted to tell you but I couldn't. Fergusson threatened to have Aileen, Ruairidh and Lily evicted. He said if I told you it would make it worse."

"So that's why you went? Not because you didn't want to be with me?"

"I wanted to stay but it would've been terrible if they'd lost their home."

He moved his chair closer and took her hand. "I had no idea. I was thinking I'd just imagined we had something good."

She shook her head. "You weren't imagining it but I couldn't think of a way to explain."

"It'll be OK now anyway. There's some good news. Wilkie called. The eagle was poisoned and the case is going to trial. They're certain of a prosecution for Fergusson this time. Menzies will probably be found guilty of culpable wildlife crime and lose his sporting licence. And Creag Dhubh is up for sale."

"That's amazing."

"It is. All because you found the eagle."

"You helped. And Marianne."

"Some people aren't happy, but most are. There's loads of ideas being thrown about. One is that we're hoping to do a community buyout. Get some help to buy the land. We want to build sustainable housing, set up some art and photography courses for visitors – that's where you come in – we're even talking about a new school. One that includes teaching the Gaelic language."

"It sounds really exciting." She was quiet for a moment,

thinking. The painful ache in her stomach had eased.

"You should come back."

She looked at him, trying to see what was behind the words, and in his eyes she saw certainty and love.

"Yes."

*

The Grants agreed that Rose could move back into the cottage by the loch. They'd installed a new kitchen and bathroom with a shower instead of the old bath. She and Tòmas decided it was too soon to live together, plus she needed the space to work. In the mornings she liked to lie in bed and watch the square patch of sky above her head change from grey to blue and back again.

She and Aileen organised a series of art and craft courses at Kinloch village hall. Rose was to teach drawing in the landscape and Aileen knitting and rag rug making. Blair was one of the first to sign up; her mum had relented and was allowing her to apply to art school. Rose said she'd help her put together a portfolio.

Rose was continuing with the clay relief. She decided it would be a memorial for those who'd lived at Torr Uaine. The design had a raised border of tools that would have been used on a croft. In the centre was some writing, in Gaelic and English, which read *Airson muinntir Tòrr Uaine. Buinidh an tir do na caidireas i.* "For the people of Torr Uaine. This land belongs to all who cherish it."

In Perth Library, with help from the genealogy assistant, Rose found a Catrìona MacGregor living in Pitlochry in 1851, in a house with Padair MacGregor and two other family members. She also found a death certificate registered in 1852. The death was recorded as

"Myocardial Failure" – her heart had given up. She was sixty-two.

The young woman was sympathetic and told Rose it was likely that Catrìona was buried in the churchyard in Pitlochry.

Tòmas stood next to Rose at the graveside, his arm around her. She laid a bunch of daffodils by the headstone and said, "I'm sorry we never met, Catrìona. You're in my heart. I promise I'll look after the graves in Killichonan."

*

That summer Rose stripped off her clothes and walked into the loch. She hadn't swum since she was nine years old; back then she'd been like a water baby, until her dad had gone under, never to resurface.

The water was cold and took her breath away. She swam out towards the middle, amazed she could still remember how to do it. She turned onto her back to look at the sky and imagined she was a dolphin. For a second the fear came, threatening to overwhelm her and bring on the panic, but then she heard a voice from the loch side singing in Gaelic. The sounds flowed across the water, over her body, calming her.

This was her place now.

She belonged.

Acknowledgements

With thanks to Lesley McDowell for her incisive mentoring, Eleanor Wood for the Gaelic tuition, and a special thanks to Aki Schilz, of The Literary Consultancy, who encouraged and supported me in the writing of this novel.

During my research I read many fascinating books about Scotland and Highland and Gaelic culture. Thanks, in particular, to James Hunter for his book, 'On the Other Side of Sorrow', and for Isabel Grant's informative, 'Highland Folk Ways'.

Thanks to Emily Mahon for the beautiful cover.

About the Author

Born in 1955, Emma Cameron grew up in Hertfordshire, close to nature, with a Scottish father and an English mother. She has a degree in Embroidery and has had many exhibitions of her art. In 2003 she co-founded the group 'Art Not War', in response to the Iraq War. After working on a memoir about her life as an artist she began writing fiction. Her letter, 'The Hawthorn Tree', was published in 'Letters to the Earth, writing to a planet in crisis,' in October 2019.

'A Scattering' is her second novel – the first was published under a pseudonym.

She lives in Worthing with her partner Rob, where she writes, paints, plays the accordion, walks on the South Downs and engages in climate activism.

Lightning Source UK Ltd.
Milton Keynes UK
UKHW011834080821
388491UK00001B/198